G000117431

DECEPTION

Also by this author

Lucid

Available in paperback and ebook formats

DECEPTION

MX Watson

Deception

First published in Australia by Insync Books
PO Box 526, The Gap, Queensland, Australia 4061
ABN: 74 087 648 600
Copyright © MX Watson 2016

The right of MX Watson to be identified as the Author of the Work has
been asserted in accordance with the Copyright, Designs and Patents Ac
1988.

This book is a work of fiction. Any similarities to actual persons, living o
dead, is purely coincidental.

All rights reserved. No part of this publication may be reproduced, stored
in a retrieval system, or transmitted in any form or by any means, electronic
mechanical, photocopying, recording or otherwise, without the prior writter
permission of the publisher.

Cover design by Insync Books

Cataloguing-in-Publication (CiP) entry:
A catalogue record for this book is available from the National Library of
Australia.

Deception
MX WATSON
ISBN: 978-0-9946164-3-2 (mm-pbk)

Dedicated to Nanny Voo

Prologue

Northern Kazakhstan/Russian Border
Location: Chemical Weapon Factory
Time: 0240

LIEUTENANT BRAD CAMDEN, *Mission Identifier: SIX*, stared ahead at the shattered monitor, horrified that his insides now coated the fractured glass. Burning pain spread out from his chest. Before the agony could reach his arms, a second bullet passed through his head. His team member, *Mission Identifier: FOUR*, reeled away from the sizzling display and pulled an explosive from her ammunition belt.

A chopper had dropped them at the outskirts of the facility twenty minutes previous, before fluttering away into the nighttime blizzard. The hushed sounds of the UH-60A Black Hawk had changed in pitch as it sailed out over the southern ravine.

SIX's legs crumpled as he landed, forcing him to tumble forward on his knees before rolling up. Bracing against the storm, he reeled in his parachute, using the gale to twist the guides between his hands.

FOUR touched down as a wind gust propelled her parachute to the side. She struggled to stand as the squall dragged her over the ground and off her feet. She pulled down the mesh half-face mask of her Gentex HALO helmet and shouted for help, but the intense wind carried her voice away.

SIX checked his wristwatch. Less than sixty seconds remained to assist FOUR, or else he'd have to abandon her and continue with the mission. He ran over and grabbed Four by her harness, and lifted her to her feet. She pushed the mask back on as the pain from the elements speared into her. Another gust blew and forced her to the ground. The tension in the suspension lines refused to yield and the canopy remained deployed. The squall intensified, knocking Six away as his alarm sounded. He had to go; the mission's success ranked above individual survival, a potential outcome they were both expected to handle.

The bitter wind was dragging Four closer to the chasm. Snow whipped against her goggles and obscured her view. If she couldn't free herself before she reached the ravine, chances were the storm would lift the canopy back into the air and fling her across the terrain. The odds of surviving without help were dismal. She looked around and found herself alone.

Her parachute then outlined a tall, thin object. Six sliced through the canopy with his combat knife, and the silk ripped apart, releasing the pressure on the suspension lines. Four spun onto her feet and pushed the disengage button. The risers snapped free and the silk rippled over the Russian steppe, lost in the growing blizzard.

"Come on," Six shouted, his voice muffled by the black material covering his mouth. "We're behind plan."

The readouts on his wrist comms unit flashed red. A message from Horus recommended abandoning the mission. Time was too tight. Six swiped away the message and urged Four along faster. Their feet pounded over the hard and uneven earth as the snow turned to a muddy slush. Arctic air bit into their lungs as they charged toward the collection of buildings that comprised the chemical factory. Exposed skin at the edges of Six's mask turned red as the wind burned through the material.

The elevated floodlights around the perimeter of the facility cast shadows of the fencing. Six and Four ran from their touchdown points to the mesh. Six extracted a micro laser-cutter and sliced through the steel wiring, then pushed open the wire and held it for FOUR. She scrambled through the narrow split, with the fence's rough edges snagging on her outfit. He picked her clothes free and she continued in. As she pulled aside one edge of the wiring, SIX pressed on the other and moved into the compound.

The blizzard intensified, layers of snow settling on the pair's shoulders and covering their tracks as soon as they made them. Forklift trucks maneuvered around the site with their spotlights sweeping through the snow, catching the white flecks in their bright beams. Each truck couriered oversized drums adorned with the standard DANGER: HAZARDOUS CHEMICALS sign between the factories.

SIX's comms unit vibrated. Two words appeared on the small display: DESTROY NAPALM. He smiled. Napalm seemed comical and quaint by today's standards.

The industry dedicated to cutting-edge chemical warfare plants spewed out WMDs without conscience or political or religious alignment. The cold data said chemists sold the product to the highest bidder. Although an inappropriate word for the situation, napalm was retro in the New World of horrific, customized, on-demand terror. Whatever the undocumented reasons for destroying places such as this, their destruction made the world a less evil place, even if it was only for the agency's benefit. SIX smiled again as he started the timer: twenty minutes.

FOUR pointed at the guards patrolling in pairs, all of who ambled between the oversized metal sheds. The guards' relaxed nature indicated overconfidence in both the facility's ancient surveillance equipment and their isolation. Scanning the compound revealed more than a dozen pairs. A nearby patrol met with another and talked, swapping cigarettes and drinks.

FOUR and SIX kept down on the ground and crawled toward

the closest building. They darted between vehicles and discarded ammunition containers, using them as cover. Six placed a Semtex explosive, labeled with the number *1*, on the casing of a fuel store. A truck drove past at walking pace, its windscreen wipers thrashing against the elements, and he and Four ducked in behind the tailgate. Red light bathed their faces as the vehicle stopped, to be replaced by a white glow as it reversed toward the building. Caught in the vehicle's lights, Four and Six ran toward another collection of drums stacked against a smaller, windowless building with two empty trucks by its side.

Six slipped under a truck and placed explosive *2* against the fuel tank. The ballet of forklifts dissolved, leaving a clear path to the central production factory. Six and Four moved in closer to the enormous tin shed and watched the activity.

The strong squall rattled the steel walls until they emitted a metallic resonance that cut through the howl of the wind. A dozen men teamed to load black boxes onto the back of waiting trucks, each decorated with the names of fake international couriers. People streamed around the loading bay in a flurry of activity.

"Can we get in?" Four asked in hushed tones.

Six shook his head. "Not through there."

From their vantage point, he pointed to a small entrance toward the rear of the building. They crept between the trucks until they had a clear view of the doorway. A glowing green sign above the entry displayed Exit in Russian script.

Two guards sat on chemical drums on either side of the door. One laughed and kicked his heel into the danger sign of his drum. The other mimed a gaseous death. Six indicated to Four to target the men. He withdrew his Spetsnaz-issued PSS-2 and Four followed suit.

He nodded three times, each movement slow and deliberate, and on the fourth they fired a series of shots. One guard thrashed his arms as the bullets passed through him. The second stood, but the silenced shots pinned him against the wall. Both slumped but remained seated on the drums as their eyes stared ahead, vacant and lifeless. Six and Four ran to the door, confirmed the kills, and wrestled the hefty coats off the men. They slipped off their outer clothing layers down to their body armor, then pulled on the coats and fur hats. The guards' AK-12s looped over their heads, allowing Four and Six to check the weapons. They searched the guards one final time before entering the shed. The next patrol was expected in fifteen minutes.

Lamps suspended high within the expansive roof of the factory shone down and bathed the entire space in a bright, brittle light. A handful of technicians glanced over as the small door opened, but returned to their duties after spotting the disguised Six and Four enter. One scanned them for a few moments before being distracted by commands shouted from the loading bay.

Four and Six approached the metal walkway surrounding the distillation and production plants. Six took in the unexpected scene. The building swelled with personnel, and any of them could blow their cover. The weight of the guard's coat concerned him. If they had to run, the bulky parkas would slow them both, Four more so. He checked his timer: fourteen minutes.

An odd scent drifted over them. Almonds. Six turned toward Four, her features masked by the huge fur hat, and whispered, "Something's wrong."

They made their way down a staircase into an excavated pit. The intensity of the stench increased. He spotted a few bodies lying against the earth walls, pale faces with blue lips. The workers in the lower level all wore gas masks. Six and Four hustled around to the rear of one of the two-story production cylinders. Ice had formed on the curved metal. Six wiped away the frost from the chemical identification sign. NERVE AGENT.

He pulled the coat sleeve up his arm to reveal the comms unit and typed, FOUND KOLOKOL.

FIND WHO IS ORDERING, Horus said.

WILCO. WHAT ABOUT NAPALM? SIX typed.

DESTROY ALL.

SIX glanced at the numerous cylinders, each towering from floor to ceiling.

"Do we have enough charges?" FOUR asked.

"Not for the whole complex. We need to be clever in here. The napalm should be enough to take out most of the tanks."

He placed explosive *3* underneath the Kolokol cylinder near the igniter, and they moved on.

Ten minutes.

The napalm unit was ancient in comparison to the modern gas-production chambers. Its orange-peeled bronze plating gave the cylinder an antique appearance. SIX placed explosive *4* under the base of the production unit. Grease and ice clung to the decades-old metal. He threw *5* to FOUR and motioned for her to plant it under a cylinder. His lungs began to burn from the ambient gasses that had built up in the pit. They climbed the stairs and exited the factory.

FOUR and SIX dragged the dead guards near the small, windowless building and placed them under the trucks. They were about to ditch the parkas when the next patrol appeared around the corner. SIX checked his wristwatch: eight minutes. The patrol had arrived early.

"Hey, what are you doing away from the door?" The guard's thick Russian accent verged on indecipherable in the high winds, and SIX's ear for the language was still crude. The patrol leader had his hand clasped around the grip of his machine gun.

"Taking a piss," SIX said as he stuck his hands in his pockets. The AK-12 hung around his neck, swinging freely.

"Both of you?"

Six shrugged. In his pocket was a small, metal flask. He pulled it out and loosened the lid, taking a sniff. Vodka. He took a small sip and offered the canteen to the patrolling men. The leader nodded and took several long gulps and finished the drink. He threw the flask back at Six. It bounced off his chest before it fell and lodged semi-concealed in the snow.

"Piss off," the patrol leader said. Six and Four walked along the patrol route, mimicking the pace of the compound's lazy and indifferent security. Once hidden from view, Six pulled out his binoculars and scanned over the remaining buildings. He pointed at a stone building with a warm yellow light spilling from its windows.

Six minutes.

He signaled for Four to follow and they double-timed across the open terrain. The building's door handle gave easily under his grip. He withdrew his PSS and wrenched the door ajar. Two guards were shot dead before they had a chance to move. A third reached for his gun. The hiss from the PSS underscored its lethal nature and killed the man with the hush of a stolen kiss. The guardroom opened into a corridor with four doors. One door creaked open and a clerk emerged. Her surprised face froze as Four's shot pierced the office worker's skull. She collapsed to the floor. Four stepped over the body and fired a second shot into a man sitting at a desk, his face a mask of horror. Six peered into the opposing room. Several wall-mounted monitors displayed the same faked footage. In four minutes, they would be switching back to the live feed.

"Keep an eye out," Six said, lowering his voice. He checked his wristwatch.

Three minutes.

Two hushed shots caught another office worker as Six crept into the next room along. The final room was empty. Six pushed the dead clerk off his seat and sat behind the terminal. Russian letters scrolled across the screen and he flicked through the directories: Purchase orders. Clients. Nothing like a bit of Russian efficiency and transparency.

"What are you looking for?" Four whispered.

"New directive," he said. "Looking for buyers."

"Anything unusual?" He caught a change in her tone and was about to turn when something caught his eye.

"Yes," he replied, the word taking several seconds to speak. He reached into his jacket for his pistol. "The records show a sizable order for Kolokol from Hydra."

"Is that a surprise?"

"Hydra is the black ops acquisition arm of the—"

The screen in front shattered and blood coated the glass. The second bullet sliced open Six's head. He slumped forward over the table.

"I know what it is," Four said. "The question is: How did you know classified information?"

Four slid her hand over the comms unit on her arm. A small group of icons appeared across the green display. She pressed out a code. Mission compromised. Six awoke. Neutralized. Proceed or decept?

Decept was the response.

Wilco.

She placed explosive 5 in Six's lap and slipped out of the building. Four let her huge coat fall as the door clicked behind her. Shots rang out. Masonry pelted her body armor as bullets peppered the wall beside her.

Her timer read ninety seconds. She sprinted toward the entrance point. Shouts cut through the wind and the lights on several trucks illuminated as their engines started. More gunfire followed. Floodlights swept over the facility. She pressed 5 on her detonator and the explosive erupted inside the stone building, its force partially contained within the solid walls. The roof flew skyward. The trucks raced toward the building, plowing through the snow. She pressed *2* and the trucks beside the production factory exploded, the blast rolling them onto their sides. The security patrols scattered in pandemonium, firing at shadows.

Four pressed *1* and the fuel tanks erupted. Glowing fire radiated out, silhouetting her. Nearby guards wheeled around and fired. A series of bullets impacted over her chest, each like the blow from a baseball bat. The body armor took the impact, but Four was forced to the ground. With her head swimming, she rolled in behind a stack of SKG ammunition boxes. Glancing over the stack, she spotted two guards now approaching with AK-12s at the ready in between her and the perimeter. She jumped up.

Tap to the head. Tap to the head. Both men down. She ran. Crashing into the fencing, Four pushed at the wiring until she found a section that flexed open to reveal Six's earlier cut. She sprinted out into the dark.

Snowmobiles roared around the outside of the fence perimeter, and lights flashed across the ground, catching her frantic legs. Another approached from the opposing side. The gorge lay ahead. They had her trapped.

A Black Hawk rose from the chasm. Bullets sparked off the helicopter's fuselage as it hovered and turned sideways. Taking longer strides, Four doubled her efforts, and leaped off the edge and soared out into the chasm.

Her arms flailed until her fingers grabbed the netting suspended from the underside of the Black Hawk. She tumbled down and seized at anything. The thick ropes slipped through her clutches until her wrist caught on the last of the rungs, nearly wrenching her arm from its socket. Her head spun as her body shot upward as the helicopter wheeled away.

Below, the chemical facility shrunk into the distance, the

raging fires illuminating the extent of the damage. Two men hauled FOUR bodily into the compartment, and she collapsed on the metal flooring.

A man wearing an all-black uniform stared down at her. "Where's SIX?"

FOUR shook her head. "Didn't make it. Shot."

She pressed *3* on the detonator and withdrew her pistol.

01

Thailand
Location: Bangkok
Time: 0020

THE LIGHTBULB SWUNG *to and fro. The room remained dark except for that swinging light. A prophecy of death: one he would welcome. The men were nothing more than gray shapes—if they were still present. They must be there. He could hear laughter, or something similar.*

He struggled to breathe through his bloodied nose. The petrol-soaked rag stuffed in his throat drove him toward suffocation. One of the guards had taped his eyes open. He hadn't blinked for what felt like hours.

And the light swung to and fro. At least he couldn't cry. The pain remained distant but would not stop.

Movement. Laughter. The room spun. Activity to his side. He heard the small metal table being dragged closer. Glass sliding on metal. A vial tapped against his temple.

"Hydrochloric acid," said the gray shape. "Say good-bye to the light."

He tried to thrash in one final desperate move, but the bailing wire tying his hands back behind the chair was too tight. The bars around his neck too stiff.

And the light swung to and fro. Out of the burning circle encompassing his vision appeared a ball of brittle white surrounded by a rainbow ring. The sphere fell toward his eye.

"They will come for you," a voice said. It was the last sentence before ... well, before things had changed.

Sean snapped back to the moment, the memory shard fading into the manic activity behind him. The rain lashed down on the windscreen, flooding over the glass and obscuring the view ahead. Headlights reflected off every surface, fractured rainbows surrounding a prism of brittle, harsh light, forcing him to blink away the recollection.

A four-by-four rammed into Sean's trunk producing a loud crunch and the old BMW rocked forward. The pickup's engine growled like a hungry beast snapping at his heels.

The wheels of the BMW skidded and bounced over the slippery tarmac as the worn rubber fought for purchase. The rear skated out toward the concrete barrier as Sean rounded onto the expressway entrance. He took his foot off the accelerator until the wheels caught and gunned the car into a long stretch on the Sirat Expressway. Bangkok shrunk away in the haze of monsoonal rain, its grimy lights resolving into nothing more than a gritty glow.

The relentless headlights appeared in the rearview mirror, rounding the onramp curve. With no place to hide on the highway, all Sean could do was outrun them.

He shifted down two gears and slammed his foot on the accelerator. The tachometer swung into the red as the old v8 screamed its defiance. The car surged ahead. He shifted into a higher gear. The tach jumped back around the dial to 5000, then 5500. Sean lurched from lane to lane as he weaved through the traffic. The cars swerved out of his way and blasted their horns as he forced his way through. The knots in the traffic lessened the farther he distanced himself from the city. He shifted again and the BMW hit its stride, leaving the four-by-four's outline diminishing in the mirror.

"Objects in the mirror may appear closer than they are," Sean said, urging the car on and away from his pursuer in the occasional short stretches of open road. Sweat poured down his forehead. Dirty-yellow ruddiness from the streetlamps rolled past, interspersed by dark patches. The rhythmic thump of wheels on the tarmac dissolved into a monotonous hum.

The garish neon of his destination to the right of the expressway caught his attention. The cascading amber of the lights reflected off the hoods of oncoming vehicles and disorientated him, but there could be no respite from the chase. The BMW's tires aquaplaned across the tarmac as the vehicle traveled too fast to maintain constant contact. He struggled with the steering wheel, trying to direct the car while keeping the momentum forward. In the passenger seat, his cell began to ring. The Captain had threatened to call to check on his progress. He took his eyes off the road to reach for it. When he looked back, he was confronted with a wall of red brake lights as the traffic slowed. He stamped on his brakes and aimed the car for a slim opening, but the wheels locked and the car fishtailed.

The BMW lost its battle, and the rear snapped around, spinning the vehicle clockwise. Horns sounded as it careened out of control along the motorway. It slammed into the side barrier, crushing the metal and demolishing the passenger doors, coating the concrete with green and silver paint. The car flipped up and over the small barrier before toppling down, tumbling into the river below. The four-by-four plowed through the other cars that had piled around the accident.

Two men dressed in black slithered from the truck, shouldering assault rifles. They shouted at the crowd, flashing their badges, and ordered everyone to stand away. The first ran to the edge of the motorway, swung his weapon around, and searched the waters below. Only the BMW's rear wheels and underside were visible as the streaming water poured around the upturned vehicle.

The second man rounded from the far side of the truck with a handheld searchlight. The bright beam roamed over the water. Automatic gunfire cracked through the air toward shadows and reflections shifting in the river. He twisted the light toward the bank, catching the final glimpse of a leg disappearing into the marshes on the riverbank. The mud erupted around the fleeing figure as bullets sliced into the wet earth.

The sounds of a helicopter grew louder. The lights shone down on the crash scene, pinpointing the men in black. They returned to the four-by-four, threw their equipment in the rear, and roared off down the motorway. The helicopter followed, its searchlights skipping over the frantic escape.

Sean closed his eyes and rested in the mud, listening to the ambient noises, people shouting, the roar of the pickup's engine, and the hiss of the river. The earth pulsed with a fast and constant beat. Music. The sounds of the helicopter rotor blades returned.

Everything was wet. He checked his gun's clip. The bullets were soaked. The cracked screen on his cell held little hope in its operation.

Beams from searchlights sliced through the rain and swept over him. He jumped up and sprinted away toward the thumping music. The helicopter spun, tracking Sean's movement through the marshland. Then he was gone.

*

Sean peered over the hood of the battered old Ford at the edge of the parking lot. Several cars away, the grunts and groans of a blond-haired man, a Western tourist, making out with a local drifted down. He hazarded a look in the couple's direction and spotted them hanging their legs out the passenger-side door of a yellow 1980s Celica. She hitched up her skirt and rode him like a sprinting racehorse. Sean paused, wondering if he should interrupt them to see if the man's clothes would fit. The guy wouldn't know Sean's gun wasn't working.

Sean rechecked the gun's firing mechanism, but it was still damp. It was approaching three in the morning; at least his wristwatch still worked. The desperate revelers and the better class of hookers would have gone. Only the drinkers and the drugged-out—the not-too-observant—would be left.

The couple continued, the woman becoming increasingly louder. This was Sean's fourth nightclub of the night. His search for Jaide Gabat had taken him all around town, one unreliable lowlife after another leading him between the clubs. He'd visited each Raven venue, and Jaide had been at none of them. Now, in a last-ditch effort, Sean was checking the most down-market club the self-proclaimed mafia owned.

He waited for the couple to finish. They had provided an entertaining ten minutes while his pistol and clothes dried. The—he assumed—woman, unfulfilled either sexually or financially, shouted at her date, or client, pulled down her bright red skirt, stretching the material to reach her thighs, and tottered on her high heels across the carpark to the nightclub. The relentless, heavy beat thumped through the walls of the old factory. Sean glanced over at the man in his retro Toyota as the guy stood behind the open door and finished off what the woman couldn't. Sean rolled his eyes.

Two bald bouncers, who were bulging out of tight-fitting skivvies, manned the front door, leaning against the wall. They clicked their counters as people circulated through the venue. Keeping beneath the windows of the cars, Sean sneaked around to the rear of the building, stacked with crates and trashcans. Among the general mess, he heard moans and spotted two figures.

A man reclined against a pile of wooden crates with his trousers around his ankles, and a woman's head bobbed away in his lap. He appeared more than a decade older than her, with slicked-back and receding hair and a pencil moustache, although he'd attempted to match the younger generation's dress sense. She wore the club's hospitality uniform with the front unbuttoned, exposing her young breasts in the moonlight. They bounced in sync with her rhythmic movements. She was probably an employee wanting to improve her career prospects with the boss, which was exactly the kind of distraction Sean wanted. Several broken crates were abandoned nearby and he picked up a loose slat and hefted it in his hand. He ran his eye along the top of the service door, spotting it had a hydraulic closing mechanism.

Within a minute, the deed was done and the young lady buttoned her top back up as the manager zipped himself away. She wiped away the corners of her mouth and straightened out her uniform. The manager swiped his card and pulled open the service door, allowing the girl to step inside. He patted her backside as she giggled and feigned shock, and then followed in through without a final check of the area. The gas chamber hissed as the closing door bounced against the pressure.

Sean sprinted across the distance and rammed the end of the wood into the opening before the lock engaged. He paused, peering through the crack in the door and calming his breathing. The manager moved through the room and disappeared out another door into the club, leaving the small storage room clear. Sean slipped his fingers into the gap and crept in, easing the door shut. One dim lamp standing in the corner illuminated the black room, revealing stacked crates, piles of lost clothes, and half a dozen promotional four-foot cutouts of popular vodka-based drinks. The dark carpet stuck to his shoes as he walked across to the room. He opened the door leading into the main space and the full sensory overload of the club hit him. Smoke, lights, stale beer, and a bass banging enough to emotionally topple anyone over thirty.

Surprisingly, the club was packed despite the late hour. The room heaved with gyrating bodies over a flashing floor that rotated through various bright colors and racy images. Sean emerged out from between two bars with bartenders so busy they didn't notice him. Sean's fashion sense and age made it obvious he wasn't part of the scene, but he might pass as a friend of the manager. He moved into the seating area adjacent to the dance floor, a series of secluded circular booths occupied by groups of lonely girls waiting for someone to buy them a drink, or couples capitalizing on the dark lighting and sparking off in the first rounds of foreplay. Either way, those activities were not what he was looking for.

A group of nearby girls on the fringe of the dance floor peeked over in his direction. At over six foot, Sean was too bulky to miss. He towered over the locals and his dark clothes clashed with the rainbow of brassy colors draped over the club patrons. It was the '90s all over again, but without the godawful whistles and glow sticks.

A commotion by the front entrance caught Sean's attention, and several police entered the building. He dissolved into the crowd. The clutch of inebriated girls who had been watching him cheered as Sean joined them. One dropped her arms over his shoulders, reaching up and pulling herself close and grinding her body against his. Her pupils were dilated. It was disappointing. Her midnight-black hair was long enough to tie back and flow over her shoulders, highlighting a flawless complexion on a delicate face defined by high cheekbones, large eyes and full lips; all exotic and intoxicating. Sean hated to see girls doing this to themselves, so loaded they could barely speak their name. She wrapped one leg around his and thrust her crotch into him. She reached up, trying to pull his head down to hers, but Sean craned around, tracking the progress of the police through the crowd. Four of them split into pairs, and skirted the dance floor peering into the crowd.

The DJ changed, tag-teaming during a long snare roll. The intensity of the beat transformed, upped from happy house into mainstream electronica. The driving rhythms and diving bass lines heightened the crowd, and Sean could swear the girl clinging to him wanted to throw her clothes off and show her grind.

Couples were climbing a dark stairway at the rear of the

venue to the mezzanine. *Couples*. The police were looking for a man, not a couple. He grabbed the girl by the waist and lifted her off the dance floor. She wrapped her legs around his waist, threw her hands above her head, and closed her eyes as her friends cheered.

He forced off her legs at the base of the stairwell. She bent down in a haze, revealing a skin-tight dress clinging to a shapely body, and removed her shoes—lacy black stilettos. The music switched to a current hit and she whooped to the chorus and danced, holding her shoes in one hand and Sean's hand in her other. He kept her between him and the police's line of sight, hoping his black clothes would blend into the background. The majority of the patrons on the upper floor were crowding around the ledge to look down onto the dancers below. A roped-off VIP area was on the right, a one-way mirror spanning the room and a stern bouncer blocking everyone. The girl leaned against the bar, standing on the metal footrest, and ordered shooters, waving two fingers.

A couple of scantily-clad women wrapped around an aging Japanese businessman exited through the mirrored door. At the back of the VIP section was an exclusive bar. Sitting at the far end of the bar was Jaide, Sean's target. He was reaching for the Beretta tucked into his belt as a commotion erupted by the stairs. The police were coming up. He grabbed the girl, who spilled the drinks over her chest, and dragged her to the first door he could see. It opened and three women with bleached-blonde hair and oversized gold jewelry walked out of the bathroom giggling and whispering to one another. He ducked into the bright room. Several girls were snorting coke off the long vanity, absorbed and oblivious to him, eyeing up their own reflections. Sean and the girl packed into the end stall. He listened to the voices rambling over inane topics, waiting for a change in pitch.

She pulled at his shirt, lifting it and exposing his muscled torso. Her fingers caressed his skin, tracing around his bulked-up shoulders over defined abs. She tucked her fingertips into the waist of his jeans, fumbling with his belt and buckle. She ripped open the fly to expose his Calvin Kleins, now apparently showing the result of the girl's affection. She pulled down his briefs and ran her fingers over him, feeling him throb and grow under her touch. In a move Sean considered far too practiced, she pivoted around the toilet seat and lowered herself onto him.

The women outside the stall let out a short outburst followed by the scurrying of feet. The girl writhed on him and moaned as she rode, rocking her head back as he pushed into her. Locks of dark hair worked loose and fell around her shoulders. Footsteps paused in front of the door. His pistol was still hooked on his belt, pressing against his back. He reached around and withdrew it. The police banged on the door. The girl shouted, cursing the policeman in a flurry of abuse. She clenched her eyes and pushed hard down on Sean, her facial muscles drawing tight.

The footsteps trailed away. The girl leaned forward, placing her arms against the wall and breathed hard. She bit her lip and arched her back.

Sean wrapped his arm around her neck and squeezed her throat. The carotid choke rendered her unconscious in seconds. Her limp body made him feel sick as he lifted her off, but time was running out. He lowered her down onto the toilet seat and gently tried to place her in the most comfortable position. He re-clothed and eased the door opened an inch.

The bathroom was empty. He returned to the VIP room. The club was still thumping. He approached the bouncer, who raised a palm and pointed away, directing Sean to the staircase down. Within a blink, Sean grabbed the bouncer's arm, twisted it around behind his back, and rammed his head into the glass door, which cracked. The bouncer slumped to the ground. Sean pushed in through the door and pulled the Beretta from his belt. Jaide paused in her earnest conversation with a Western gentleman, either Russian or Baltic, and glanced in Sean's direction.

A heavy hand landed on Sean's shoulder, intercepting his path toward Jaide. Slipping the gun in his pocket, he spun around, dropped to his knee, and uppercut the security guard in the crotch. The guard doubled over in pain. Sean spun him around and pushed the guard into the path of a second one, a younger and nimbler man. An obvious punch came in, and Sean ducked under and around, coming up on the outside of the swing and planted a combination of blows that ended with a hook to the man's temple. The guard collapsed, and Sean spun around and drew the Beretta.

Jaide smiled and mocked him with slow handclaps. Sean flicked off the safety without hesitation and aimed the pistol. The wall beside him exploded as a bullet narrowly missed him. The glass wall shattered, and the broken shards rained down. Music screeched to a halt.

"Put the gun down," screamed a policeman.

Sean raised his hands and lowered his head as he turned.

02

Ireland
Location: Banbridge
Year: 1993

"HEY, SEAN, YOU want another pint? Your mates are having one. I'll spot you."

The room spun as waves of nausea rolled over him. The

26

smoke stung his eyes. Sean's friends cheered as, possibly-Mickey downed another pint. Their chanting floated over the general noise in the pub. His brother had disappeared in a place with nowhere to hide. Sean checked the booths and the toilets again. "Jesus, me ma will kill me."

"She'll have seen worse. After all, she had to put up with your da."

Sean's temper flashed. "You don't know him."

The neatly dressed man smiled. "You're right. I hardly know the drunkard who couldn't pick the winner in a one-horse race."

Sean tried to remember what he knew about this man. Jack said the bloke's name was Liam and was a friend of his brother, down from Belfast. He spoke to the gang, individually and in depth, as he plied them with pints. He talked about cool things, stealing stuff, fights, running from the police. He asked if they were involved in anything. What they thought of the English and Americans. And Sean regurgitated the typical shite that the gang talked about.

Liam spent longer talking to Sean, and now he found himself in the dilemma of having a lost sibling. His mother *really* was going to kill him. She'd been so protective of them since, yes, the drunkard had walked—or staggered—out the door. And they'd been forced to move, for unsaid reasons, from their home surrounded by fields to this shithole of a city.

Liam adjusted his thick glasses and checked his wristwatch. He'd been doing that for the last half hour. A waitress arrived with a pint. Sean sat down in the booth and continued to scan the pub. Liam offered him the glass.

"You want your pint?"

Sean took a sip from the glass.

"Get it into you," Liam coaxed.

Sean took a longer gulp. The irritation from the smoke intensified. His head hurt and the dizziness increased. "I don't feel too well."

—the glass on the coaster swirled. Everything in his vision shuddered—

—the glass was empty—

"What was that?" Sean asked.

"Maybe you need some fresh air. You're looking a wee bit pale."

—the door shut behind them—

—Sean vomited over the wall. He rested his head against the bricks—

"Ain't that your brother?" Liam said.

"Where?"

"Being attacked by that gang."

"Jesus, no," Sean shouted.

"Don't just stand there." Liam's seemed different, more aggressive and commanding. "Go help him."

The world blurred and went dark. All Sean could see was a boy landing blow after blow against his brother's face. He ran forward screaming.

And Liam stood by and smiled and nodded.

*

Thailand
Location: Bangkok
Time: 0218

A plastic bag and a thick file bristling with Post-it notes dropped on the desk in front of Sean. A police captain, as designated by the three stars on his shoulder, in his mid-forties sat down opposite. His dark hair was cropped close. A tightening uniform showed a relaxed approach to middle age, although his skin held the usual local magic that disguised his years. He pulled the Beretta from the plastic bag and smiled as he twisted it, then placed the pistol on the table facing Sean. He extracted a black, metallic wristwatch from the bag and raised his eyebrow as he spotted the Rolex insignia. The remaining items included a Mont Blanc pen; the latest iPhone with a cracked screen, which failed to turn on; and a leather wallet with an American Express Centurion card. The captain laid out all the items across the desk, examining each. Eventually, he glanced up at Sean.

"I am Inspector Dumo. Would you like to tell me your name?" The inspector had a deep, smooth, and resonant voice, full of authority. Dumo's English fluency implied he'd spent considerable time overseas. He gave Sean a fleeting smile, exposing a set of coffee-stained teeth.

Sean said nothing. The featureless interrogation room in the ultra-modern building reminded him of unpleasant places he'd visited and put his nerves on edge. The marks on the utilitarian walls and floors attested to the forced methods of information extraction. Dumo stood and examined Sean's clothes. He ran his fingers over the material and around the collar. He stepped back and continued.

"Your license says Simon Reanne. What do you do in our city, Mr. Reanne, that requires you to carry a gun while wearing such exceptional designer clothes and upmarket accessories?"

Sean remained impassive and stared ahead at the desk. The inspector slid the file across and opened to the first page. He glanced up at Sean before returning to reading the information. He flicked through the many pages. Dumo sat and reclined in his seat.

"Immigration states you are a French national"—he waved the sheet—"for three years. I assume you can speak English. It says you speak English."

Sean sat there in silence, staring at the metal table and watching the ceiling lights bounce off the shiny but pitted surface containing knife marks, scratches, and small spots of blood. Inspector Dumo examined Sean's face for any emotion.

"Simon Reanne is a business analyst. Apparently, it's a highly competitive occupation. Simon Reanne also has no work visa. So how does a business analyst support himself and his excessive lifestyle with no visible financial support?" The policeman leaned forward and stared into Sean's face. Sean could detect an accent, possibly American. "You have a distinct scar under your eye, like a tear. I hope they are not tears of a clown."

A younger police officer, barely more than a cadet out from Sam Phran, knocked on the door to the interview room. Dumo switched to Thai. The young man recounted an unofficial eyewitness statement describing his target. Dumo turned, catching Sean listening in on the conversation.

"You certainly speak something, Mr. Reanne. Due to the nature of such things here, people are scared of saying what happened, but you were in a venue owned by the Raven syndicate." Dumo paused and waved the police officer away. "Some are saying, unofficially of course, the daughter of Harry Gabat, Jaide, was there, and you were pointing a gun at her. Harry Gabat is an old and sick man and has run the Ravens for many decades. It would be terribly unfortunate for them if the new leader was killed as she was about to take over running the operation." He smiled, tapping the folder.

"Of course, for us, this is a good thing," Dumo continued. "One less drug syndicate, especially the largest one, would ease our workload and make the city a better place. But I doubt you were there on our behalf. So, whose?"

Another young officer appeared, this time recounting a manic chase through the city out toward the club. Dumo smiled again as he glanced over to Sean.

"You are going to prison, Mr. Reanne. There is no escaping it." The lights flickered, and Sean's eye twitched. The inspector's voice drifted away. "And men like you don't …"

Voices, always coarse voices, shouting and snarling at him. Pinned against the prison wall, a knife to his throat and hateful words spat in his face. Provo. Catlick. The beating had gone on for days, or what he assumed was days. Being pounded into unconsciousness as soon as he recovered made time meaningless. They had battered him until they broke their own fists on his bones. But they couldn't finish him, or he wouldn't let them win. Mortar flecked and crumbled as they pushed his bare back along the bricks toward the embedded blades. The torture's intensity had increased as special instruments had been swapped, stolen, or traded. They were going to finish him.

Then there had been the voice. It boomed from above with might and power beyond understanding in his delirious state, followed by the punch that equaled it. The attackers fell away, crumpling under his power, dissolving into the broken light his crippled vision could barely discern between eyes so badly beaten. And the voice said, "You're one tough fucker."

"And what makes Mr. Reanne sweat in such a cold room?" Dumo clicked his fingers in front of Sean's vacant stare. "Does prison hold a particular fear? If so, you are going to love it here."

Sean snapped back to the moment, jolting in his chair. The handcuffs rattled. Three police appeared, two with M4 carbines.

He checked the cuffs chaining him to the table: ASP chains, double-lock channel, and stainless steel. Cheap, but reliable and hard to release. The policemen were young, inexperienced, and edgy. With dozens of men in the building, chances of escape were poor. The Captain was going to be unimpressed if he had to bail Sean out.

*

Sean's cellmates crowded around him, pushing him against the bunk bed and hissing derision. They struggled to abuse him in English, but as soon as he responded in the local dialect, they flared. Upon reflection, he shouldn't have made the comment about the assembled group's odor. To insult them was one thing, but in their own language was a deliberate and provocative statement.

"You fucking understand me, whitey?" the head of the cell dwellers growled.

Sean raised his hands, attempting to defuse the situation. The three other men leered at him, tensing their muscles.

"No offense meant," Sean said. "My mistake."

"You got a funny voice there, snowflake. Where you from?"

"Which bunk do you want me to have?"

"You sleep on the fucking floor."

Sean shook his head, to the shock and disbelief of the men. "I don't think so." He looked over his shoulder and sat down on the lower bed, laying out. His full height took up the complete length of the small bed and his feet hung over the end. It was a continual annoyance in these prisons. Apparently, no one over six foot committed a crime. He squirmed on the uncomfortable mattress in the scratchy prison clothes. Under his feet were some of the men's stowed belongings. He kicked them off the mattress. Two men leaped at him, grabbing his arms and legs, as their leader whipped out a butterfly knife and stabbed it into Sean's stomach, causing him to cry out as the stinging pain speared into him. They pulled Sean off the bed and flung him against the wall. The two men held his arms back as the leader confidently waved the knife in front of his face.

"What the fuck you thinking? We cut you open. Teach you some respect." The leader stepped up and placed the blade against Sean's temple. The man's body odor nearly made Sean gag as he stepped in close. As the knife blade glided over Sean's skin toward his eye, sweat trickled down his face. Blood seeped out of the wound.

"You don't like it. You afraid now, big man."

The blade touched the corner of Sean's eye, pressing down and pulling it into a slit. With lightning speed, his hands ripped out of the sweaty grip of his captors and drove into both sides of the leader's neck, crushing into the short man's carotid arteries, making him stagger back with bulging eyes, clutching at his throat. Sean smashed his elbow into the head of the man on his right, ramming it against the bricks. He then spun around, catching his remaining captor's head in his left hand, and planted his fist in the center of the man's face. The nose cracked and the cartilage shattered into the man's brain. The lifeless body collapsed. To Sean's side, the leader struggled to breathe. One step at a time, he moved toward the man, backing him against the bunk beds. His terrified expression had no effect on Sean. The leader held up a shaking hand, loosely holding the knife in a way that was somewhere between a delusional threat and surrender.

Sean grabbed the leader's head by his cropped hair and wrenched it backward. He ripped the knife from the man's sweaty palm and plunged it into his throat. Sean pulled out the knife and blood spurted all over the wall. He let the man and knife drop to the ground, both bouncing off the stained concrete at the same time.

He held his hand to the wound in his gut and grimaced. It stung despite its shallowness, but the blood stopped him ascertaining the extent of the injury. Sean rummaged through his cellmates' belongings, knocking them out of the small lockers onto the floor, eventually finding a contraband bottle of cell-distilled bourbon and a crude medical kit. He had to wonder what the items said about the prison. The clear liquid's scent had him reeling as he poured it over his wound, washing the blood away. Examination showed the small incision had barely pierced his muscles and cut nothing major, but still needed to be stitched.

Nothing looked clean, except for his own prison-provided outfit. He removed his top and held it against the wound, but it failed to clot. He fumbled with the first aid kit and found a suture pack. Several mouthfuls of the bourbon numbed him enough to insert a couple of rough stitches and slap on a plaster.

The men crumpled on the floor provided a problem. He didn't want to lift them onto their bunks in case his wound reopened, and he certainly didn't want to sleep on any of their bunks, which were filthy and probably teeming with microscopic life. Maybe the floor was the best place to be. He laid the men across the floor and slipped his mattress on top of them. It was marginally more comfortable than the iron bed frames which, he noticed, had deliberately twisted springs poking up.

It was an exercise in excess, but if nothing else, it made him look like a total badass, something insane that might earn him a bit of respect while inside.

*

A pitcher of water splashed over Sean's face, waking him. He struggled to piece together a sentence as three guards hauled him up off the mattress. They smacked a set of cuffs on his wrists, and a baton was thrust against his neck forcing him into the wall.

"What the hell went on here?" a guard demanded. He kicked aside the mattress revealing the dead bodies underneath.

"One tough bastard," said another guard. Another baton smacked into Sean's back. He checked his wound. It was holding. The first guard pulled Sean's other wrist behind his back and slipped the cuff over his wrist.

"What's going on?" Sean asked.

"You got bail," the guard said as he and his comrade pushed

Sean out into the passageway.

"Who?"

"By the favor you do in the cell, my guess is the chief." The guard laughed, and pushed Sean along, punching the end of the baton into the small of his back. But not too hard.

Within the hour, Sean had been hosed down, his injury properly dressed, and his clothes returned warm and clean. Dry cleaned. It was better service than his last fleapit hotel in Cairo. The drugs were probably better, too. The quartermaster handed over his belongings. Sean slipped on his Rolex and checked the time. 07:00. Someone had bailed him out before six. No one he would have been expecting.

As he signed out his belongings, Inspector Dumo appeared with one of the young officers from the previous night.

"Mr. Reanne. We meet again."

"Inspector."

"He speaks!"

Sean half smiled. "Sometimes."

"You have a wonderful, gravelly voice. I am sure the women love it. You should speak all the time. Especially when being asked questions by the police."

"Who bailed me?"

Dumo glanced over to the quartermaster, who checked his records before replying. "Tom Whistler."

Dumo nodded. "Yes, that was the name."

"Who?" Sean asked.

"You have an interesting—and certainly not French—accent. Almost musical."

"We should spend some time together, then."

"Ah, you have wit. Or at least half of some."

Again, Dumo displayed more intelligence than Sean had encountered in the local force. Dumo stepped over to the enormous steel door, which clicked loudly as the lock released.

The door swung open and Dumo offered the outside. As Sean passed, the inspector grabbed Sean's arm and looked up into his impassive face.

"Mr. Reanne, try to stay out of trouble."

Sean nodded and continued out into the early morning. Dumo and the young officer watched him leave, hesitating on the pavement before moving off to the left.

"Did you mention how Simon Reanne had been killed in a motor accident in 2010?" the officer asked.

Dumo shook his head. "No. I think this Simon Reanne might be helpful. He will be a breeze drifting through a deck of cards. Let's see who will remain."

"And does Mr. Whistler know he is also five years dead?"

The inspector sighed. "The Americans have no respect for the dead."

*

"You!"

"Surprised?"

"Not the word I'd use, Robo," Sean said. "Or is it Whistler?"

Tom Robinson held out his hand.

Sean hesitated before shaking it. "Is it booby-trapped?"

The lanky American in ostentatious sunglasses had been leaning against the entrance of the police station and Sean had caught him scanning the area. The passing traffic was minimal this early in the morning, and the tree-lined park opposite was empty. Tom checked his wristwatch: 0715. "We've got ten or fifteen minutes before HQ works out you are here."

"How'd you know I was in this dump?"

"They scanned your mugshot, and our facial recognition software picked you up," Tom said. "Try not to use an ID of someone who's been dead for five years, you dumb paddy."

"I didn't need your help."

"You're not acting very grateful, considering I just bailed you out and have given you excellent career advice."

Sean laughed. "I assume you're here to arrest me. Out of the frying pan into the fire."

Tom paused. He removed his sunglasses and stared into Sean's eyes. "I got bad news. Camden went down."

Sean stared his feet. Sorrow flooded over him. It wasn't always inevitable, but it did happen. Brad Camden was a top operative with a handful of bad breaks. But the agency had always placed their faith in him because, basically, shit happens.

"I know you were friends," Tom said.

"What happened?"

The American surveyed the area. The street was packed with nondescript cars parked down both sides. "Walk with me."

They crossed the street into the rows of trees circling the park. Shadows from the leaves danced across the tropical grasses as a breeze rustled through the branches.

"He was stepping out and got a pat on the back, according to the body armor sensors. Seventy-five kilometers to the southeast of some shit hole called Prigorodny. Too dull to have a landing strip or a strip club."

Sean sighed. The assassination of an agent was always disappointing, especially in the back. But of all the situations and combat missions, a simple infiltration should not go wrong. "Who was the eye?"

"Me. Mission code: Horus."

"Funny."

Tom glanced around the trees, searching down the line of cars. He leaned against a tree trunk and signaled for Sean to move in close. "Something is up. They buried him on site. You'll see it in the news … well, the explosion at least."

"Who was with him?"

"This is where it gets difficult. We set up the mission last week. I organized Frank Jensen to run as 'Four'. You ever met Frank?"

Sean shook his head. Tom took out a folded piece of paper and handed it to him. Sean opened it and read the summary. Frank Jensen's body was found, washed up on the West African coast, three days ago. He glanced up at Tom.

"Someone was watching the missions, killed Frank, and slipped someone else into the position. The mission records still have his name, but I know it wasn't him out there."

"For sure?"

"I've ran for Frank in the past. I know how he works. This wasn't him. Someone with about half his strength."

"That's most of us."

"This is serious. I was communicating with Brad as designated lead. He said he'd found stores of a nerve agent when our records said there weren't any. This stuff is expensive and made to order, so I told him to see who was ordering it. I tracked Brad's trail across the facility, but the camera feed was flakey. He was sitting at the freaking terminal getting the info then the line cut."

"You sure he wasn't caught?"

Tom shook his head. "Four detonated an explosive at Brad's last known position. Then, when on the chopper, set off an explosive taking out the napalm but leaving the nerve agent. *Leaving* the nerve agent after I said destroying it was a priority."

"Who else knows about this?"

"That's the thing. No one was meant to know about it. But someone, Mr. X, was watching. Mr. X intercepted the comms, *then* he deleted them. I lost comms with Four the moment before Brad's signal died until he was outside the facility. Locked out for about four minutes watching Four run, watching Brad die, unable to say or do anything. Then the whole thing disappeared before my eyes."

Again, Tom looked around, his eyes darting through the shadows. "But what no one knows is I read the lines before the secure overwrite."

Sean lowered his head and clamped his lips.

"*Mission compromised. SIX awoke. Neutralized. Proceed or decept?*" Tom related. "The last instruction was 'decept'. Then the place blew."

"'SIX awoke'? I don't get it."

"You're right, it makes no sense. First up: SIX awoke. Brad found out something he wasn't meant to, something that would compromise a mission, but not my mission. You know what neutralized refers to, so the implication is that FOUR shot him. Look, the mission was to blow the place. The deception would be to *not* blow it. FOUR had orders that contradicted mine from someone who could override me and have the authority to delete—not redact—classified records, as if they never existed. Whoever was playing FOUR was getting a clashing set of orders from higher up than me."

"You can't find out who?"

"Records deleted. Helicopter disappeared off the face of the planet."

"What about the pilot?"

"He was off register. But now he's recorded as MIA in '08, although I spoke to him last week. More records changed." Tom shrugged, before looking down the street once more. Several cars drove by. Sweat beaded on his forehead. Nervous tics. Unusual and impatient speaking pattern.

"You're off grid," Sean said.

Tom nodded.

"When did this happen?"

"Last night. 0240 local time. Your face came up on the scan while I was chasing down the deleted data, and I caught the first flight."

Sean stepped away and scanned the park. A young couple had appeared, a toddler swinging between their arms. A jogger bobbed by. The hum of a waking city started to intensify. "You brought them to me."

"Chill. I deleted the facial scan and secured the mission files before I came. You got time. They won't know why I'm here."

"One of them will. Mr. X."

"I'm sorry," said Tom. "But I need your help."

"What do you want me to do about it? Last time I checked you wanted me dead."

"Not me personally, except for that time in Mexico when you left me in jail. You know Brad's girl, don't you?"

"Yeah, Amanda. She's nice. Kept him calm. We go back a few years."

"Get her to a safe house. She may know something, overheard conversations Brad may have had. Anything. I can't do it, because as soon as they work out what I'm doing over here, they'll come down on whomever I've been in contact with. We need to keep her safe. She is our best bet at the moment."

Sean gave Tom an unimpressed stare. He shook his head. "I can't help you. Especially after what the agency did."

"I understand. I'm not asking you to bring down the largest intelligence organization in the world. Only to check on Amanda and get her to the safe house."

The two men stared at each other. Sean couldn't read any telltale signs of deception. Tom was a snake, slick and always twisting. But they had history, some of which had been fun, and the agency had higher profile targets than him to chase.

But even as a pet, a snake was always going to bite you. Each step needed to be careful.

"For Brad? We need to find his killer, Mr. X, especially as it's internal," Tom pleaded.

Sean paused before nodding. "Not for you or any other

individual from the hellhole, but for Brad. And if I feel them crawling up my back, I'm cutting free."

"Call me when she's safe. Have you got a clean phone?"

"Ah, no phone at the moment."

Tom tore a piece of paper from the bottom of his e-ticket and scribbled down a phone number. He folded the paper and handed it over the Sean, who slipped it into his back pocket.

"Sean, not everyone is your enemy."

"It feels like it."

"You didn't have to run."

03

SEAN STOOD WITH his head lowered as the diminutive man bellowed at him. The Captain was parading around the expansive colonial office in his immaculately pressed nautical suit and comical sailing hat, gesticulating wildly. The culture conflict of empire against his Thai heritage was farcical, but people didn't laugh for long when this madman had a weapon in his hands.

"It was a simple task. Shoot the stupid bitch. I use to do it all the time. Sometimes for fun. You start as scum. You kill the target. You get to the top. Simple. You fail to kill the target, you stay scum. Of course, I, like Charlie, never failed a simple task."

Charlie sat, relaxing on a long bench seat with his legs spread, his broken teeth jutting out from his evil grin. One knee bounced incessantly as the Captain spoke. Charlie's scarred, bald head reflected the afternoon sunlight spilling in through the French doors. Both his arms stretched along the back of the bench, his right hand holding a Scotch glass, ringing the bottom of it around on the bench material. The ceiling fans hummed away, keeping cool air circulating in the humidity.

Rodriguez Manus—the stocky, dark-skinned head of security—stood to the left in a sharp gray suit, clasping his hands in front. Rodriguez's eyes flicked between Sean and the Captain. A small garden lay outside, through the French doors. Bright sunlight filtered down from a clear sky into the paved area, with the light catching the decorative spikes around the cast iron railing.

"It got complicated," Sean explained.

"Were police involved?"

"I used a fake name. No one is aware of our connection."

The Captain threw up his hands. "At least that's something. Can anything be salvaged from this mess?"

Charlie cleared his throat. "We push into the ghetto. Show 'em a bit of stick." His thick Cockney accent seemed out of place in the opulent room.

The Captain smiled and waved his finger in the air. "Again, masterful thinking by Charlie, seeking opportunity in the failure of others. You see, Sean, it's not difficult."

Charlie raised his glass, swirling around the ice before knocking back the remains.

"I understand, Captain," Sean said.

"Charlie says you come with many skills, but all I see is trouble and mistakes. Is that why you are no longer in army?" the Captain asked.

"I was never in the army."

"Legion. Whatever you call it. I can't believe the bitch is not dead. She has more lives than a cat. Show me something smart that saves situation. Show me why I should bother keeping you."

Sean stood straight, with his hands clasped behind his back. The Captain's head barely came to Sean's chin. "She'll be lying low. She understands we can get close to her when she goes

42

out, and that'll get her running scared for a while. Maybe take out some of the production houses they are trying to take over. If you get her reeling back, she won't have the momentum to develop the Ravens' new industries. You can offer them stability when she is clearly struggling."

The Captain paused. He then smiled and clapped his hands.

"That is good. Very good. You need to watch it, Charlie. If he thinks like that, he's going to take your place." The Captain laughed.

Charlie smiled back and nodded. "He'll keep me on my toes, indeed, Captain."

"What was the reason for this? Were you distracted?" the Captain pressed.

Sean nodded. "I've had some bad news about an old friend. He was KIA. Last night."

"It can happen to anyone."

"Not to Brad," Sean said.

"Ah, your friend Brad, Brad Camden?" the Captain said.

"Aye. I'm surprised, and honored, you remember him."

The Captain smiled. "He was the soldier? We had dinner at your house a few years ago. He had the girl who sat next to me."

"Amanda."

"Yes, that her name. She was delightful. It is sad news. What happened?"

"He was assassinated by his own people on a mission, then the records were destroyed," Sean said.

"Can they do that?"

"Generally not. But it shows how untrustworthy the CIA can be."

The Captain smiled. "Have the afternoon off."

"Thank you, Captain."

"We talk tomorrow about how to kill the bitch. And, Charlie, you can implement Sean's clever idea while he mourns his friend."

The Captain removed the cravat from his neck and wiped away perspiration. He waved the damp cloth toward Rodriguez. "You stay. We talk, then train." He dismissed the others and reached for his Seidokaikan equipment, his daily training being the predominant reason the man had remained so fit and fierce. Charlie stood and stepped in behind Sean as he exited out the office's grand double-door entrance, spinning to close the great doors. The antique wood thumped together, the weight echoing down the spacious hallway. The metal lock fell into place, and Charlie's face turned dark and menacing.

He hurried to catch up with Sean, who was briskly walking toward the entrance of the Captain's palace. Charlie's footsteps were silent on the marble floor. He waited until they were out of the Captain's hearing before pulling a long knife and thrusting it against Sean's throat, pushing him back until a chaise stopped the momentum.

"I got plans, I do. You'd better not stand in the way or get any ideas above your position, or I'll cut your fucking head off and piss down your throat."

*

The information scrolled across the displays in the logistics room and was met by a sea of stunned and disbelieving faces. Sandra Henderson turned to the intelligence officers. The small room was overcrowded with rows of desks and fresh-faced intel clerks who radiated confusion. She'd been tasked with a low-key observation, something for them to sink their inexperienced teeth into, to get them into the habit of running information between the temporary room and the head's offices. An air conditioner, failing under the heat of an early morning Los Angeles summer, spat and spluttered. Henderson fanned herself with a loose folder, but sweat dotted her forehead and ran in streams down her back. The heat shortened her temper. She wiped her brow and slicked back her tangled honey-colored hair.

The displays were populated with headshots of field agents. Henderson pointed at the top right monitor; an outline of Thailand with the audio wave of the transmission rolled out beside it. Below the wave was the codename of the contact: Two.

"Is this for real?" she called out to the assembled staff. "Authenticate the transmission. Check the files on Camden— his last known location, last mission, recent contacts and phone calls. What's going on at his house? When did he call in for training or anything? How are we only finding out about this now? Where did the information break?" She threw an empty folder on the desk closest to her and pointed at it. "Fill it."

Hands of the dozen officers scuttled across keyboards, trawling through the audio. Henderson walked around the desks with her hands on her hips, keeping an eye on the monitors, pausing in front of the only fan they had in the room.

"Play the audio again." The muffled and hurried voice rattled off the security code, then disturbing information. Sandra pointed at the linguistics expert. "What the hell did that last bit say?"

"I'm on it, ma'am."

"What's your name?" Henderson glanced down at her badge. "Verity Palmer. Verity, get me some traction on the audio. Are you good at the tech side?"

"Best in the room, ma'am," Palmer replied as she looped the last few seconds. She ran the audio through a parametric equalizer filtering out the noise. Another clerk called out.

"Call delivered through the secured gateway, ma'am. Voice and security code match. Transmission verified. Only problem, it's not a scheduled call."

"So what we know is this is our agent, Two, who is nervous enough to break protocol and call us. Confirm if the transmission information is true. Is Camden down? Is the information first or secondhand? Get any supporting evidence. Check news sources. Pull up the mission data. Who's playing on Two and who's the eye?"

"It's a level-one mission. Data is restricted."

Henderson tapped her fingers. "See if there are any listings in the RCOMS."

"The what?" the clerk asked.

"The records of commands breached database. All active missions must keep a log of any breaches for internal audit. This mission is still active. If Two has been a problem, then it will be recorded."

"Nothing in the database," the clerk confirmed after a moment.

Palmer raised her hand. She had an earphone from her headset pressed against her right ear. She glanced around and gave another set to Henderson. "You need to listen to this," she whispered.

The audio played on repeat until Henderson's ear tuned into the phrase. *Mission records were deleted.* She stood in silence as the clerks amped up one another. She leaned in close to Palmer.

"This is security level one, Verity. Lock it. You did not hear it, and you will talk to no one else about this other than me."

Palmer nodded and typed a phrase. The audio wave disappeared from the screen. The energy in the room increased as the chatter between the officers buzzed and the conversation bounced from one side to the other.

"Ma'am, breaking story from Al Jazeera. They've run a short piece about a fertilizer factory exploding last night out on the Russian border. Not many details." The clerk brought up the

Al Jazeera web page on the central monitor. She highlighted the story and enlarged it to fit the screen.

"I find that an improbable coincidence," Henderson said. "Check the name on the piece."

The clerk zoomed in on the byline. "Mosa Al Saad."

"She's the Eastern European and Russian security correspondent." Henderson paused. "Odd person to cover something so insubstantial."

"Is it a cover?"

"Print it. I'll check."

The clerk slipped the folder into Henderson's spare hand. She flipped open the cover and scanned down the brief text. The copy didn't make sense. It was the only news item covering a potential agency incursion, and the press loved this stuff. They had a missing agent and an explosion, yet it was covered as an environmental incident. Mosa was smart. Henderson could rely on her ability to see through it.

"Where exactly on the Russian border? Get me the coordinates. Call Mosa. Give her some incentive. Someone check the mission log and see if we had anything planned at"—she glanced down at the name—"Prigorodny. Or however the fuck you say it."

The buzz momentarily lulled as the staff absorbed her unusual expletive.

"Wait!"

An image appeared on the display. It was blurry and at an odd angle. At one side of the picture was a tall man wearing all black. A red square highlighted his face. Several names scrolled past as it flashed agency photographs against the enhanced image.

"Who is Sean O'Reilly and why is his name flashing on the screen?" Henderson demanded.

A laser printer hushed into life, and several pages scrolled out. The clerk swept them up and slotted them into another folder. The details were surprising.

"He's one of us?" Henderson asked.

"Was, ma'am," the clerk reported. "Records show he's rogue. Dishonored."

"People, we have a rogue operative working with a number. Alarm bells should be ringing. I don't like the silence." Henderson reached over to the folder being offered by the officer and paged through it. "And this is everything?"

The officer nodded.

Henderson shook her head as she reached the last page. "It doesn't add up. Leave this with me. I'll speak with Banks. Hopefully, we won't all be fired or dead by the end of the day."

She made her way out of the logistics room along the dull corridor to the office of Clive Banks. Henderson peeked in through the venetian blinds. The section head sat back, reading the morning paper. He sipped at a coffee as he slowly turned the broadsheet, his thick, slicked-back gray hair and jolly, round face belying the severity of his authority. Henderson knocked on the door.

Banks glanced up over the paper. "Yes?"

Henderson entered and stood in front of his desk. "Intel from Thailand. Our operative has a surprising update." She slipped the folder on the desk. Banks placed his coffee down on the newspaper and opened the file.

After he had read the first paragraph, Banks glanced up at Henderson. "Unscheduled transmission from covert source. Agent Camden is allegedly down on an off-the-books mission? Possibly a hit on an alleged chemical weapons out in … Prigorodny. Who authorized this and when did it happen? Who was the eye?"

"Tom Robinson," Henderson replied. "He's part of the answer. Hopefully, he can supply the rest of the information."

"When is Robinson due in?"

"He's scheduled for tonight."

"You called him?"

Henderson nodded. "No answer. Phone is cold and currently in his house."

Banks nodded while biting his top lip. He closed the file and handed it back to Henderson. "Pull him in when he arrives. We'll both speak to him. Who is the operative out there?"

"Two."

"Do we have a name?" he sighed.

She shook her head. "Only the eye has that information."

"Who's the eye on that?"

"It's a level-one mission. We don't have access."

"Jesus, Sandra. You're meant to bring me solutions."

"I'll see if I can track it down, but we'll need your authorization to get anything."

"Has Two been reliable?"

"From what we've been able to ascertain from the records … He has been in the past."

"Fine. Pull info on Camden. See if he has anyone close we can lean on. A wife? Girlfriend?"

"Amanda Sakda. You met her last year at the Christmas party."

"At this point in time, Ms. Sakda is part of the situation and we need to retain objectivity. What do we really know about her? Get someone down to stabilize the situation. Also, get a team down to investigate Amanda's home." Clive looked at the file again. "And who is Agent O'Reilly when at home?"

"He's a rogue agent. Went bad a couple of years ago. It's the first we've seen of him since he left," Henderson reported.

"He's not Two?"

"No."

"That'll be all unless there's anything else?"

49

Henderson hesitated and mentally bounced the last piece of the recording. The last part of the transmission said that comms got deleted. Only someone with high-level clearance could do that. Someone like a section head. At this point, she didn't know who she could impart the information to until she found solid evidence.

"Can we have authorization for the level one mission?" Henderson asked.

"I'll see what I can arrange."

"Sir." She turned and left.

"Close the door behind you," Banks called out.

Henderson smiled and pulled the door handle until the latch clicked. She hesitated for a moment, wondering where to explore next. She'd been given an instruction; it was important to be seen to be following orders. She headed to the logistics office.

*

Banks watched through the blinds as Henderson walked away. He questioned whether having an ex-IA person had been a wise choice. Once she was out of sight, he picked up his phone, double-checked the door was closed, and pressed the top left button on the keypad.

"Yeah, Clive here. Do we have a problem in Prigorodny?"

04

S EAN SWORE. AMANDA'S address and phone number were on his dead phone. He'd have to go home to pick up the details off his laptop. The local corner phone shop was doing a brisk trade. He picked up a cheap Nokia, discarded the packaging, and inserted a new sim card. As it searched for a network, he pulled the piece of paper in his pocket from Tom and stored the number in the phone's memory. He then scrunched up the paper and threw it into a drain.

The streets were coming alive as the heat and light of the day ebbed away. People shouted and waved at him as he passed through the thin alleys to his small, off-grid apartment. Despite the high-class furnishings, the apartment had no phone, television, or radio. No hints he lived there.

Two policemen milled around in plain sight outside the apartment. They chatted to the younger ladies wandering by, smiling and calling after them, to the exclusion of all others. How did they find the place? Sean ducked around the corner and leaped up onto the opposite building's fire escape. He pulled himself up until his feet reached the rungs of the ladder and scrambled up to the rooftop. He paused to assess his options, not wanting to risk the three-story drop between the buildings, before backing up several steps. A couple of quick strides and he sprang over the gap, landing and rolling.

His feet smashed into a small wall on the far side of the building, stopping him from continuing over into the drop. He grabbed the roof edge and lowered himself down until his toes reached the ledge of his window.

Squatting down to open the window, while balancing on the ledge, he eased the wooden frame up enough for him to drop his legs inside then slip on through, landing on the polished floorboards without a sound. The lounge appeared untouched. He crossed to the hall and caught the outline of the police officer through the mottled glass. The lock was secured and the junk mail lumped on the floor indicated the door hadn't been opened.

Sean entered his bedroom and pulled open the bottom drawer in his dresser. He slid open the drawer's concealed base to reveal a compartment. The dark lining covered half a dozen loaded clips for his Beretta and a fistful of cash. After slipping into a clean set of clothes and checking his wound, he grabbed the cash and ammo and slipped them into various pockets. He hefted a laptop resting on the bedside table in his grip, assessing its weight as he made his way back to the lounge window. Traders and customers passed by below, colorful shade cloths lined the street. No one stood out as suspicious. He slid the laptop into a backpack and started to zip it closed.

He caught the sound of a faint click, causing him to pause. A high-pitched buzzing started, followed by the clicking of a rotary dial. He glanced over his shoulder. Sitting in the center of the coffee table was an ornate Balinese cat sculpture, rocking its paw back and forth. It was new and out of place. He leaped toward the window as the statue exploded. Fire erupted, engulfing the room as he crashed through the glass.

Sean's laptop tumbled out of his pack and fell the three stories down, shattering on the ground, as the blast blew him across the small alley and smashed him into the opposing wall. The impact knocked the wind from him and he tumbled down, falling through the canvas awnings shading the windows below, slicing them open as he fell to the street.

Residents shouted out as Sean landed hard. He staggered to his feet. Several men ran toward him; not police. He scooped up the remains of his laptop and sprinted off in the opposite direction. Shots were fired, followed by screams. The bullets tore through the air, ripping holes in the wooden buildings. He ducked around a corner and ditched the smashed remains of his computer into a food vendor's fire, the sizzling meat spitting as his hands grazed under the hot plate. He concealed himself in a doorway behind a hanging sheet, listening out for running footsteps.

He heard someone's manic approach, stepped into the street and swung out his arm, catching one man across his throat.

The man twisted in the air, partially somersaulting before landing headfirst on the concrete pavement. A punch then landed against Sean's lower back, and a high kick came in from the opposing side, catching him across his head.

Sean tensed his stomach and raised his hands to defuse another barrage of attacks. The first attacker drew a knife and lunged at him. Sean caught the man's arm and twisted, plunging it into the chest of the second attacker. Sean whipped out his Beretta and fired a single shot into the remaining attacker. The gathering crowd stood in stunned silence. They knew him, a quiet tenant who was considerate and often helpful to his neighbors. Now he was and would always be the killer on the street. He fled, leaving the peaceful neighborhood behind.

*

He couldn't remember the number or name of the road where Brad and Amanda lived and had to rely on a collection of landmarks. They lived on the edge of the *faran* sector, on the eastern side of the Chao Phraya River. He remembered crossing the Krung Thon Bridge. Their house was an old empire residence dating back to the fall of Ayutthaya.

It was night by the time he hit Ratchaphruek Road. The lights were reflecting off the tarmac, made shiny from a brief downpour. The continual flow of traffic hummed past, causing Sean to blink back the discomfort of the headlights. He hailed a taxi and directed it across the Krung Thon Bridge. Cars flowed around and behind the cab as the driver weaved through the traffic, but no one appeared to be tailing them. Sean directed the driver down the streets taking cues from the many landmarks dotting the area. Another downpour swept over the city, forcing the driver to turn his windscreen wipers to maximum. Headlights from oncoming cars refracted through the water, irritating Sean's vision. He indicated for the driver to pull over into a

Shell petrol station, not wanting to give away his destination to anyone who may be following.

He tipped the driver and exited. Under the canopy covering the petrol station's driveway, he watched the cars pass by in the rain, splashing the puddles over the pavement. After five minutes, he felt comfortable that no one had followed him, certainly not into the petrol station. Sean lifted a counterfeit New York Yankees cap from a rack in the forecourt and pulled it down to conceal his features. He made his way down the backstreets toward Brad and Amanda's house. The alleys were empty except for the occasional car parked half on the street, half on a driveway. A handful of streetlamps cast weak light on each block. The rain continued to pour.

He approached the house, the memory of it now familiar. An eight-foot stone fence with swooping cutouts enclosed with iron bars surrounded the property. Wooden double gates stood chained closed in the center of the street wall. Sean peered through the narrow gap between the gates into the courtyard. The light from the streetlamp didn't reach the house, obscuring it, and concealed the courtyard and veranda in darkness. He walked along the wall to the lowest cutaway, jumped and lifted himself to the top of the wall. As soon as he landed on the broken courtyard tiling, he sensed a problem.

Sean stepped through the decorative garden, letting his eyes grow accustomed to the dim night light. His footsteps were silent as he stepped up the wooden stairs to the veranda. The drumming of the rain echoed on the roof, and the gutters gurgled as they overflowed. The house felt empty. He knocked on the door. No answer. He tried the handle. Locked. He hesitated as he reached into his backpack for his lockset. Breaking into his friend's house bothered him, but his concern for Amanda overrode that. Sean knelt in front of the ancient lock and speared the two thin metal pins into the slot. Twisting the two into alignment, the locked clicked and the door eased open, creaking as it moved.

If he'd known for sure if Amanda was home, he would shout out, but the quiet and dark kept his movements stealthy.

He reached for the light switch, but nothing happened when he flicked it on. He stepped into the room, closing the door behind him, sinking into the gloom, and listening for any noise. *Boyfriend dead. House quiet. It's not adding up to good news.*

He pulled out his torch from the backpack. The LED beam flickered on, dancing over the disarray on the floor. Books and overturned chairs lay scattered on the floor. A broken vase in the corner. Dirt from indoor plants crunched under his boots. He pulled out his Beretta and pushed off the safety.

The next room revealed the same destruction. Shattered plates and toppled dining chairs lay on the floor, but no sign of blood. He climbed the broad stairs, which split and circled around to an upper foyer. He'd spent a dozen nights crashed out in the second bedroom when he'd come back late from a mission with Brad. That lay to the left off the foyer. Amanda's and Brad's room was to the right. He crept over to the door. It opened without a sound. The bedroom was in disarray. Someone had searched for something important.

The light revealed drawers pulled open, with clothes scattered over the floor. He followed the trail of clothing which led to the couple's California king four-poster bed. The netting was ripped down, the pillows slashed open. And in the middle of the mess was Amanda. Her dried blood, trailing out of her nose and mouth, had stained the sheets. The assailant had torn open her clothes. Sean reassessed the destruction of the room, correcting his thoughts. Someone had gone to the effort to make it appear incompetent thieves had looted the place.

Sean sat down next to Amanda and swept back the long, dark hair from her face. She was still as beautiful in death as she had been in life. The face of an angel, the heart of a saint. She'd shown both him and Brad deep understanding and compassion, and this situation was unforgivable. By his estimation, she was three hours dead, give or take half an hour, placing the murder between 1730 and 1800. He leaned forward and sniffed, catching a faint scent of perfume. It wasn't Amanda. He followed the fragrance.

Roses were scattered under the bed. He pulled the broken bunch and examined them. They had been expertly tied with a thick red ribbon, but had been trodden flat. No card or note. Just a dozen red roses. Red roses, a dead girl. Her wrists also showed bruising and cuts. He'd have to check. He closed his eyes, apologized to both Amanda and Brad, pulled up her skirt, and gave her an examination. Evidence of sex. Bruising. His anger boiled. Who would send her roses straight after her boyfriend had died?

He sat back and leaned against the headboard.

"Okay, Brad, you wouldn't leave her alone, unprotected. What did she have access to?"

Sean examined the cornices around the ceiling. No obvious cameras. The picture frames had been pulled off the wall. A photo of Brad rested on its back by the bed. Sean pulled off the back, revealing a micro camera embedded in the frame. Brad was always keeping an eye on her. It couldn't save Amanda, but maybe it could avenge her. The wire from the camera ran around the rear of the frame to a fake slot for a wall hanging. Sean pulled out a pen and pressed into the slot, and an SD card slipped out of the base of the frame. Sean held it up, examining it, before slipping it into his coin pocket.

Over the high fence, a car rolled down the alley with only its parking lights on. It stopped in front of the house. A man in a dark suit got out and sparked a cigarette lighter, taking several puffs before wandering down the street. Sean moved over to the window, watching the man's movements. Two men had remained in the car, sitting in the backseat. Sean's senses switched into overdrive. He doubted he'd have minutes if they were here for him, but who were they with? He turned and let his gaze drift over the room.

"Start thinking, Sean. Amanda is confronted by someone. The most significant information she can share is her phone," he said. He stood at the foot of the bed. "You're standing here. A man comes in. You have a phone. How do you conceal it?"

He glanced back out the window. The men in the car were still there.

"Quick. Quick. Man in front. Phone. Can you hide it behind your back without it being obvious? No. So, you turn, holding it in front of you." He mimed clasping the phone in front of his stomach as he had seen her do during his visits. He scanned the various angles of the room. "Can you go by the bed? No. Can you move to a different room? No. But you could walk to the window."

He leaped back over to the large framed window. It wasn't locked. He blinked. The men were no longer in the car. He scanned up the street. Below, the aged floorboards by the door creaked, and he heard the lock being forced. The silhouettes of two men appeared through the gateway, shining torches across the courtyard toward the front door. The light reflected off an object in the flower pot below. He stepped away out of the main view of the window and glanced down. The light caught the edges of a phone. Confirmed.

"Clever girl," he whispered.

The men had spread out and were stepping up onto the veranda. In the stillness of the night, he heard the creaking of their clumsy footsteps, and the delicate clicks of their weapons being primed. *Did they know he was here? Of course, why else would they be here?* He sneaked out to the foyer. Muffled voices bounced up from the lower level. He descended the stairs to the landing, taking aim over the balustrade, waiting for the first target to appear. If they weren't grouped together, the situation was going to get difficult depending on their weapons ability.

He quietened his breath, regulating his breathing as he kept both hands gripped to the Beretta. He could take down one, that was easy; and if he could get a clean shot at the second, he might be able to run through the door before they could have a chance of returning fire. But grabbing the phone in time would be a challenge.

An outline of a leg moved into his field of view. He locked onto the movement, waiting to target a vulnerable part of the mark. The second leg appeared. A waist, stomach, and finally the chest. Sean squeezed his finger against the Beretta's trigger, and as he was about to pull it home, sirens ripped open the night. The men turned and charged out of the house. Sean dashed down the stairs after them, watching them pile into the car. They started the engine, only to kill it and duck as police cars flooded into the alley.

Neighborhood lights turned on as the residents emerged to investigate the commotion. Flashing blue lights lit up the street as three police cars pulled up to the front of the house. Sean plunged his hand into the flower pot and pulled out the phone as the gates opened. He charged back into the house as police swarmed into the courtyard. The headlights from the police cars flooded the yard, finally illuminating the extent of the destruction within the house.

Sean knew the floorplan well. The property was hemmed in on three sides, leaving the front, through the police, as the only possible exit. He ran up the stairs, turned on the landing, and sprinted up to the foyer as the police entered the building, spreading out into the lower rooms. Sean entered the guest room, locking the door and sliding the chest of drawers across, blocking the way in. He crept over to the window and peered through the closed blinds, gently parting them between his fingers. Sean shielded his eyes from the bright headlights. A familiar figure followed in behind the police team. As he stepped forward, the light peeled away and revealed Inspector Dumo.

Sean swore under his breath. Then he noticed the car with the first three men was still there.

Shouts rose from the foyer, and the guest room door rattled. Half a dozen men were working through the courtyard garden. Sean flipped open the latch on the window and opened it an inch. He aimed and fired two shots. They smashed into the window of the three men's car. The engine roared into life, and the car shot down the alley with its tires squealing. It crashed its way through the parked police cars before skidding onto the road.

Half the police in the courtyard turned and ran back to their cars, quickly taking off in pursuit. Sean pushed aside the blinds and fully opened the window. Crawling up onto the window ledge, he leaped up to one of the solid eaves and swung over to the fence running beneath the roof. He gained his balance and ran toward the alley along the top of the wall just as several more police charged out of the house and started to fire at him. Jumping off the fence, he landed out in the alleyway, diving into a roll and sprinting away down the street.

*

Dumo glared at the officer. He was losing patience with the young man's inexperience. The officer had trouble speaking his own language coherently, let alone getting his thoughts in any kind of order. "Omid, do we know who the men in the car were?"

"No," Omid replied. The junior officer presented in a pristine uniform, his dark hair smoothed impeccably to one side

"Do we know why they were here?"

"No."

"Do we know why they were shot at?"

"No. But we got the plates. That should lead us to something."

"Don't pin your hopes too much on that." Dumo glanced down the alley. The street was now full of the residents, peering at him cautiously. There would undoubtedly be complaints to the police chief. Dumo wished the man would show a bit more backbone to the foreigners. Give the police back some of the lack of respect they gave to the locals. He watched a handful of men charge after the ultra-fit assailant. "Don't chase on foot when you have a car. You'll never catch him."

"Do you know the man?"

"He called himself Simon Reanne yesterday. I assume he wouldn't have a reason to change it."

One of the police cars drove quickly down the alley as people hurriedly stepped out of the way and back into their homes. Dumo's phone rang. Head office. He sighed.

Dumo pointed Omid in the direction of the house. "Put together a quick summary while I take this."

He turned his back to the commotion around the house, blocking one ear. "Chief, I'm at the location. The trail has led to an interesting place." Dumo glanced back at the house before staring back out at the nearby big brand high-rise hotels.

"Yes, between the St. Regis and the US embassy ... I don't think it has anything to do with the Raven attempt last night, although we have spotted someone similar to the person we arrested ... No, a foreigner ... French. But not with a French accent ... No. There's plenty of intent, but no success. Chief, who is enquiring about this?"

Dumo held the phone away from his ear as the abusive tirade came down the line. He hung up, disinterested in the insecure ramblings of his senior. Omid appeared by his side.

"Tell me what you've found."

"The place has been smashed up, and there's a dead girl in the bedroom upstairs," Omid replied, licking his lips. "The property is being rented by Brad Camden. He's a US national, working for an undisclosed government organization. You think he's CIA?"

"They could hardly spell it out any louder. In fact, if they said CIA you'd find it less believable."

Gunshots rang out over the buildings.

The radio buzzed as panicked voices shouted the situation. Man down.

05

SEAN SPRINTED DOWN the alley. Someone shouted as he charged by, but no one tried to stop him. Distancing himself from the police was his priority, but he wouldn't have long before they grew tired and started shooting. He ducked around two corners and emerged onto a dual carriageway. A petrol station lay on the opposing side and a major mall to his left. Both would offer real protection and chances to slip away. He picked up his pace, choosing the mall. He'd run almost fifty yards when a familiar black sedan drove past with two bullet holes in the windscreen. The car shuddered to a halt and steered up onto the pavement.

The sedan's rear door opened and a heavyset man, dressed all in black, leveled a pistol and fired. Sean dived to the ground and rolled behind a bus shelter, but the man tracked his movement and the metal and glass of the shelter twisted and shattered. Sean rolled and took another two shots at the car, hitting the passenger window and causing the man to duck for cover. Another man on the far side of the car stood and returned fire. A police car bounced out of the alley, its engine roaring and lights flashing. The police screeched to a halt, trapping Sean between the two vehicles.

Sean scrambled and ran out across the road in between the traffic. Horns blasted as drivers slammed on their brakes to avoid him. Gunfire broke out behind him and he slid over a car's hood and watched the firefight. The car's driver switched between Sean and the danger before shouting at him and racing away. Aggravation from the motorists continued to escalate until, interrupted by the scattergun fire, the shouts turned to screams. Security fencing surrounding scaffolding erected between the lanes blocked Sean's escape route over the partition and onto the opposite side of the road. Several shots from the henchmen forced him below the eyeline of the passing traffic, watching the men to keep as much moving metal as possible between them.

Two policemen opened fire at the car. The three men returned the police's shots, winging one and sending him spinning to the ground. Another policeman on foot rounded the corner and fired back at the three men. The closest target collapsed, clutching at his throat. The farthermost man pulled out a semiautomatic and fired in a wild arc, forcing the police to dive for cover. The remaining henchman dragged the fallen man into the car. The semi's magazine ran out of bullets, and the driver smashed the car into reverse and squealed away as the passengers struggled to slam the doors closed. The car bounced onto the road with vehicles screeching to a halt as it fishtailed up the street.

A construction truck's wheels locked, skipping to a halt, with the rear wheels sliding sideways under the heavy load. Smoke poured off the tires, as the odor of the burning rubber permeated the air. A motorcyclist stopped, narrowly avoiding crashing into the swinging trailer of the truck.

Once on his feet, Sean ran to the motorcyclist, pushing him off the bike, then revved the 250cc two-stroke and took off down the dual three-lane highway in pursuit of the black sedan. Shots rang out behind him, forcing Sean over the vegetation lining the center island and into the oncoming traffic. He swerved around the vehicles as they came to a screeching halt, sounding their horns and flashing their headlights. A police car appeared alongside him on the opposing strip of the highway. One of the policemen used the loudspeaker to caution him in Thai.

"*Pull over, or we will take urgent measures to stop you.*"

Sean slammed on his brakes, and the police car shot ahead before it could replicate the maneuver. Sean veered off to the right and gunned the bike down Chit Lom Road to face four lanes of oncoming traffic. He skipped the bike onto the pavement and raced along, dodging around trees, tables, and pedestrians.

Traffic slowed the pace of the pursuing police car. Sean steered the bike back onto the road and cranked the throttle, keeping close to the curb. Ahead were the Khlong Saen Saep and the low-rise Chit Lom Bridge over it. If he could get over it then work through to the expressway, he'd be clear. But as he approached the rise to the bridge, two police cars came racing toward him.

Clutch. Drop to first. Pull brakes on full.

The rear wheel of the bike locked and skipped sideways as Sean leaned back, fighting the momentum trying to launch him over the handlebars. He twisted the throttle and jumped the bike off the pavement and onto stairs leading down to the walkway by the river.

The tires bounced and slipped their way down the concrete steps, colliding with the handrails until he landed heavily at the base of the stairs.

Click into second. Twist. Third.

The vegetation whipped against his face as he powered along the river. Couples scrambled to get out of his way, some being forced to jump into the water. Another bridge lay ahead. He ducked down, squeezing under the bridge supports, and slammed on the brakes. The rear wheel bounced around, pivoting the bike, and Sean accelerated up the stairs and onto the bridge. He pulled out onto a narrow single-lane alleyway. Small, traditional stores who weren't particularly friendly to police lined the passage. They kept quiet as Sean shot past.

He burst out onto Petchaburi Road, accelerating between two worn-out hatchbacks, the second swerving to avoid Sean and crashing into a taxi. He rode the bike under the overpass ramp to the other side of the road, which had far less traffic. Still, the sirens rang around him. He weaved around the sporadic cars until he hit the reason for the quiet road. It was blocked.

A pileup congested the intersection, as a red MX5 had rear-ended a brand-new Toyota pickup. The driver was leaning out his window and shouting at the old lady in the sports car while waving his fist. A traffic policeman in a fluorescent orange jacket was trying to calm the situation. Sean slowed the bike, revved the engine, and dropped into first gear. The front wheel lifted and landed on the hood of a car ahead of him. He accelerated, and the bike tracked over the vehicle, bounced onto the Mazda and over the Toyota pickup, until he landed back on the road. The policeman turned in amazement then ran toward him, blowing his whistle.

Sean veered right into an alley packed with pedestrians. The policeman jumped out of the way as the bike slid around the corner, its rear wheel fighting for grip. Piercing whistle blasts caused Sean to glance back over his shoulder. The policeman was running behind Sean, reaching for his radio. Shouts from in front focused Sean's attention back to the street and the pedestrians slowing him. He honked the bike's horn and shouted for them to move.

Scooters piled high with multiple sacks of produce veered out of the way. Directly in front of him, a pickup truck slammed on its brakes, and Sean crashed into the truck's rear as he desperately pulled at his own brakes. He tumbled forward into the truck bed and crashed against the cab. The policeman fought his way through the crowd, disappearing between the throng of people. Sean climbed onto the truck's roof and bounced on the hood before sprinting down the street. Shouts behind him increased and joined with the piercing whistles echoing all around him. At the end of the alley, a police car pulled up and policemen climbed out and ran down the alley. Behind him, the traffic cop was fighting his way through the crowd. Above him was a fire escape. A stack of wooden crates leaned against the wall. He waited for the crowd to swell around him. One foot on the crates, and up.

The police collided into the traffic cop, forcing the bystanders aside. They searched the area. Sean was gone.

*

Sean pulled himself up the final rungs of the fire escape. Dressed in black, above the lights, the police hadn't seen him disappear. He scrambled over the rooftops toward the northern residential sector of the suburb. Slipping down to the streets, he grabbed a 750ml bottle of water from a distracted street vendor and guzzled it. Within ten minutes, he was knocking on the penthouse door of an old acquaintance.

The apartment only lived up to the optimistic label of penthouse because of its size and spectacular view over the neighborhood surrounded by five-star hotels. Inside, it was old and grubby. A run-down and shambling place that had only ever seen one occupant.

"Hans, I've got a phone I need some info from. And can you read this SD for me?" Sean handed over the phone and card to the aging German who had answered the door.

Hans looked Sean up and down. "Hello to you, too. I assume you're not out on a late-night run."

Hans then examined the cracked cell phone as he beckoned Sean into the apartment. The screen was broken, and the edge had been smashed. He pressed the power button, but nothing happened. "This'll take a while. You can inspect the SD card in the meantime. Would you like a drink?"

"Just a chilled water, if it's not too much trouble," Sean replied.

"Still not drinking?" Hans asked.

"What kind of man would I be if I broke a promise?"

"Sobriety isn't a mandatory requirement for facing your past." Hans smiled as he replied.

Sean patted the German on the shoulder and moved over to the long workbench that took up the entire wall, cutting off half the view out of the expansive windows. "I've never told you the full story."

"If we had a drink you could tell it to me."

"Trust me. I'm better without a drink."

"Suit yourself. I'm still having one." Hans slipped the phone into his shirt pocket and moved over to an antique dressing table, which doubled as a bar. Bottles of every shape and color packed the shelves. Hans poured a three-finger whiskey shot and put on some classical music in the background. "Do I need to ask who this phone belongs to?"

Sean didn't answer. He took a seat at Hans' wooden workbench, the bench's rough surface catching his clothes. The workbench stretched the entire length of the room. Sean slipped the SD card into the reader on the side of a MacBook on the bench and a white disk icon appeared on the computer's screen.

Sean clicked on it, revealing a .mov file. QuickTime opened as he double-clicked the icon. The picture was grainy and only captured a frame every three seconds. The camera covered the bed and window of Amanda and Brad's bedroom, but only a partial view of the doorway. The movie file was of a twenty-four-hour period. A timecode counted off in the top left corner of the movie window and whirled through the hours as Sean scrubbed through the footage to locate timecode 1730, her potential death.

Amanda had crawled into bed at the start of the footage, like a bad cartoon fantasy, twitching from side to side until the morning sun illuminated the room. She wore fitted lingerie that highlighted her hourglass figure. Her hair remained immaculate even with the humidity. Then she was gone, a brief snapshot before she disappeared out the bedroom doorway. The room remained empty, with only the shadows flittering across the walls as the sun made its way across the sky. She returned, with her phone to her ear. *Who is she talking to?* "Hans, how's that data extraction going?"

"Hmm? Yeah. It's …" he replied without turning his attention to Sean. Hans hunched over the far end of his workbench with the components of the phone extracted and spread out. A faint hint of smoke coiled up from a soldering iron sitting in its holder.

Sean returned to the footage. Amanda had turned to face the doorway, giving him a clear look at her face. He paused the video and zoomed in. Her clothes were the same, except she now wore a scarf. She didn't appear upset. She probably didn't know about Brad yet. Then her head was tilted, and the phone was no longer by her ear, but clutched in front with both hands, concealing it. Sean smiled. Clever girl. Someone unwanted was in the room. Why else hide the phone?

What happened to the scarf? She hadn't been wearing it

when Sean found her, and it hadn't been in clear sight.

A new figure entered the frame, offering the flowers he's seen strewn on the floor. The angle of the camera only caught the back of the man from above. Sean couldn't even gauge his height; although, from the obscure angle, the man appeared to have a slim build. Unfortunately, that equated to about two-thirds of the population. The footage played on. A second man appeared, much bigger than the first with much wider shoulders. But again, Sean could only see his back and slicked-back dark hair.

The image flickered, and Sean leaned back before he scrubbed through to the end of the footage. Some morbid curiosity was drawing him to the kill. It made him question his own past, as he'd seen this kind of thing happen the world over. But when it happens to someone you knew, somehow it brings home the vile nature of the act.

The heavyset man watched on as Amanda threw the flowers at the thin man. She and he struggled, the thin man showing a remarkable amount of strength as he pinned her down. He slapped her countless times, which explained the blood coming from her nose and mouth. Then he strangled her with the scarf.

Amanda's body relaxed and her arms fell away, then she lay motionless on the bed. Sean wiped sweat away from his forehead as his blood pressure rose. He clenched his fists as the thin man dropped his trousers and jumped on top of her. As the last pumps of her heart would have been pushing the blood through her veins, she wasn't technically dead, but the line was close enough. The rapist was depraved on all levels, and Sean couldn't believe someone would do this to someone he knew, a friend. Sean's arm snapped out, smashing an empty vase on a nearby windowsill. Hans paused and looked over before returning to his work.

"I'm sorry, Amanda," Sean said. "We failed you."

There was going to be a reckoning with this murderer. Sean scrolled back to the point where the image had flickered. Sean pointed at the screen. "What's this mean?"

"Radio interference," Hans replied. "Someone's cell emitted a signal. Could be checking for email by 4G or receiving a text. But whose phone is it? There are three people there. Maybe even a neighbor." He followed up with a helpful shrug.

Sean resumed the footage. "Wait." He pointed again at the image on the monitor. The second man was now holding his phone, checking its screen. The next frame the phone was gone, presumably back in the heavy man's pocket, and he was staring back at Amanda. Her killer had pulled the scarf free and was smelling it before he placed it in his pocket.

"Find the scarf, find the killer," Sean muttered.

Hans took a sip from his glass and peered over the rims of his spectacles at the laptop screen.

"I thought you were going to get me a water," Sean said.

The German rolled his eyes and disappeared into his kitchen. Water splashed into a glass, and Hans reappeared with a dripping tumbler. Sean was toggling the footage back and forth around the scrambled frame. Hans hesitated as he watched, allowing Sean to spot him over his shoulder.

"Thanks," Sean said as he grasped the water glass.

"You knew her?"

"Yeah."

"I am sorry for you," Hans said. He walked back to his section of the workbench and put his back to the screen. Then he suddenly turned around, his eyes lit up, and he pushed Sean off the seat. Hans stared at the image and clicked his fingers. "Connect the RME unit up to the oscillator."

Sean searched through the equipment scattered across the tabletop. He found the units and ran a cable between them. Hans pulled out another laptop and opened it next to the first.

69

He ran a cable between them. A collection of wires looped around the back of the new laptop. He launched an audio analyzer and dumped the frame into it as a single file. He pressed a green on-screen button, and the image began to replicate on the second laptop. The speakers started to squeal, jumping randomly through the audible spectrum. Sean covered his ears in reaction to the offensive sound.

"What the hell is that?"

"It's recreating the signal the camera caught," Hans explained.

"Why?"

"You want to know the phone number of the thug in your video?"

*

"It will take a while to perform the match. Talk to me while I work on the phone."

"Can you turn the noise down?" Sean said, squinting from the aural discomfort.

"It's not noise. It is information, beautiful and pure."

"It's noise, and it's doing my head in."

Hans turned down the volume until the screeches and barks were barely audible above the classical music. The distorted image crawled across the screen, pixel by pixel. They both sat around the disassembled phone. Hans sipped at his whiskey while running a mounted magnifying glass over the components. "What trouble have you got yourself into?"

"Do you remember Brad?"

"Your friend? I don't think I met him, but you have talked about him."

"Brad and I have known each other a few years now. He joined the agency not long after I did. I took him along on his first missions. He was good. A bit strong-willed, but you get that with the new guys. They all want to be Rambo."

"Was he the reason you left?"

Sean sighed. "Part of it. We had a mission go badly wrong. He was young and had no chance of understanding the situation, and wouldn't have survived. So I let them capture me."

"Who?"

"Al-Qaeda."

Hans put down the component he was inspecting. "But that would have meant torture."

"I've been through worse."

"Than torture in the hands of Middle East radicals?"

Sean shrugged. "There are different kinds of torture. Inside and out. I can deal with outside pain."

"Not if they cut off your head."

"I can't comment. I've done the same thing, but for money, which has got to be worse than for a cause."

"Age is making you reflective?"

"The death of my friend and his girlfriend is."

"You really need a drink."

"Trust me, I don't. What do you think got me into this situation all those years ago?"

"You still refuse to talk about your youth?"

Sean sipped his water and said nothing.

Hans shook his head. "Then pass me the solder. And fill up my glass."

Sean grabbed the tumbler and refilled it from the whiskey bottle on the dresser. He looked through the window at the traffic streaming by, endless lights twisting their way through the veins of the city.

"Why aren't you still with the agency?" Hans called out.

Sean continued to stare out the window. "Their view of the proceedings differs from reality. I've been compromised. Usually, when they think you're untrustworthy, they find a permanent solution to the concern—one that can't be argued against

71

because you can't disagree when you're six feet under. If you know that little fact, you don't want to hang around."

Sean returned to the workbench and placed the tumbler down by the elbow of his friend, who smiled and took a long sip. Hans flipped a switch on a small blue box, and the abstract collection of app icons from the phone appeared on an old monitor.

"Ah hah! What information do you want?"

"Can't I take the phone with me if you put it back together?"

Hands shook his head. "This is the end of the line for this thing. Once pulled apart, you can never put it back together again. It's operational for now, but the circuits will be fusing due to the extra current going through them."

"Can you dump the phone calls, texts, and e-mails?"

The digital screeching in the background peaked and came to an abrupt halt. Hans clapped his hands together and moved in front of the laptops. His fingers danced over the keys on the second laptop, which started to count down a long series of numbers on the screen. One by one the numbers stopped flickering and stabilized. Sean found himself holding his breath as the phone number decoded from the EM static revealed itself. Within a minute the laptop displayed the completed number.

"I'd love to know how you did that," Sean said.

"Trade secret," Hans replied. He couldn't stop smiling. "Type the number into the geolocation transmitter, and place the dish out the window."

"The what?"

"Reverse triangulation. I need a satellite feed."

"No idea what you're talking about."

"Just put the dish out the window."

Hans launched another program that brought up a map of the world. It quickly zoomed into the city, with a red ring circling around. Sean forced open a window and placed the small dish out on the ledge. He then returned to the workbench, where they watched the screen as the ring began to constrict. The map continued to zoom in, occasionally jumping to random locations across the city. It focused and quickly shrunk down to a single block. A single building. A single side. Hans pulled up an isometric image of the building.

"Somewhere in there. We've got the building number, but it could be in any number of apartments."

"I'll find it. If I can get the phone dump, I'll get out of your hair."

Hans printed out the address and handed it to Sean, who folded it and slipped it into his backpack.

"I've got nothing to store the phone information on," Hans said. "Will a hard copy be okay?"

Sean nodded. Hans cued up the information and sent it to the printer, which started to hiss out the sheets.

"Hang on, can you make a call without the number signal in it?" Sean asked.

"I have a masked line."

Sean held his breath. "Can I call Ireland?"

Hans slid over an aging gray handset. "Dial zero first."

Sean closed his eyes and dialed the number burned into his memory. The phone on the other end rang. Checking his wristwatch, it would be mid-morning. She'd be awake. The repetitive purring was interrupted by a click on the line, and his heart leaped into his mouth.

"Hello?" came the elderly female voice from down the line. Sean took a deep breath and framed what to say.

A loud banging erupted on the door. Hans returned his attention back to the cell phone. "They must have been looking out for it."

Sean closed his eyes. He'd been so close, and it physically

73

hurt him to replace the receiver without uttering a sound. "We need to go," Sean said. He pulled the German toward the window. The pounding grew louder as boots smashed against the wooden frame.

"You go that way," Hans said. "I've got better places to hide in here."

"No, you should come with me."

"I'll be just as safe here."

The pounding on the door increased and was followed by a gunshot. Hans turned and nearly disappeared before Sean's eyes as a concealed trapdoor appeared beside the bar. The last thing Sean saw was the laughing German slipping down out of sight, clutching the bottle of whiskey. The door blew open and four men dressed in black ran in. Sean turned and charged toward the window, clutching at the papers coming out of the printer. The sheets spilled from his fingers, tumbling across the floor.

Sean paused to pick them up, but the intruders gave him no chance to retrieve the papers. He dived through the glass, which shattered as bullets punctured it. His body jarred as he landed on the external fire escape. He kicked down the ladder and slid toward the street five stories below. He'd lost the crucial information.

*

Inspector Dumo pushed away the folder. The information was of such poor quality, he'd found little after two hours. It had been a day of questions and not one answer. Dozens of police had chased the foreigner, and none of them had laid a finger on him. He'd floated through them like a ghost and disappeared. Dumo knew they weren't ever going to be a match for an elite operative such as this man, but he was behaving in a disturbingly non-operative way. Why try to kill Harry Gabat's daughter?

Why break into that house? Was it a coincidence about the dead girl? Did he kill her? Was there a connection to the Ravens? How had the tall American known about the incarceration? His experts were poring over the pages they'd recovered from the German's penthouse, but nothing relevant had turned up yet.

"Who are you, Mr. Not-Simon Reanne?" Dumo asked himself.

Now his boss was ringing with more questions, related to ability and behavior. Overly tense questions disproportionate to the incidences.

Omid and Jenna appeared at his office door and knocked. Dumo lifted his head out of his hands, fatigue wracking his body and mind. He wiped his hand over his bleary eyes and stared at the young officers. They looked so small and frail compared to the man they pursued. So innocent. About as far away from an operative as you could get. *Operative?* He pointed to Jenna.

"Do we have a list of dishonored agents who may be living here? Does Interpol have any details?"

"I'll check," Jenna replied.

Dumo waved Omid into his office, folding his arms and leaning forward on his desk. "Tell me what you found. Did the neighbor say anything?"

"He overheard the girl, Amanda, speaking to someone around 1730, in what was an unusually loud voice."

"Do you normally speak like so formally?" The inspector shrugged. "We have breaking and entering. Murder. Sexual assault. Strange men sitting nearby."

"The man known as Simon Reanne was seen entering the building."

"Really? Who saw him?" asked the inspector. "And was it possibly at 1730?"

Omid looked down and nodded. "A street vendor said she could place him there at that time."

Dumo laughed. "I bet she could. What do you think the chances are of finding that vendor to verify this? I'm sure she'll either have disappeared never to be seen again, or will turn up dead. It's too convenient to have an eye witness in such an unusual location."

Dumo scribbled the times on the sheet of paper covering his desk that made up his calendar, then tapped the pen tip on the numbers, lost in thought.

"Our Mr. Reanne enters at 1730, and we see him leave at … what, 2045? So, what was he doing for all that time? The girl wasn't much of a conversationalist during the period. Either he got there at 1730 or at 2045. Unfortunately, I'm finding the first time a little hard to believe."

"Maybe he was looking for something, or forgot something."

"From what I know, men like him don't *forget* anything. He's ruthless. We know this from the jail cell. Why would he start a shouting match? No, I'm thinking someone else was there at 1730. See if you can trace the call or pull the details. Also, get me the history on the address and who lived here, past and present. I should say come back when it makes some sense."

Jenna came rushing in with a folder. She placed it on the desk in front of Dumo.

He looked up at her expectantly. She opened the folder and pointed at the picture. "Mr. Reanne entered the country three years ago, correct?"

Dumo nodded.

"This man was captured by al-Qaeda three years ago. They put his face up with the other alleged soldiers they said they caught trying to assassinate the leader."

"Yes, I remember the story. Al-Qaeda pushed that propaganda piece about captured US soldiers far and wide."

"All but two of these men have returned to the USA, according to our contacts. The first is Brad Camden, whose house we were at earlier. My source hinted that he was still operating. The second …" She revealed the next page. It was an exact match. A screengrab from an old CRT display, but there was no mistaking the face and body, especially the fresh scar under his left eye. Their fugitive.

"We need to find out his name," Dumo said.

Jenna allowed herself a smile. "I already know. It's Sean O'Reilly."

06

CHANCHAI PULLED ASIDE the curtain and peeked down at the street. Headlights flashed by. Every passing pedestrian fell into his *suspicious* category. He drummed his fingers, which were wrapped in surgical gloves, as he waited for his phone call to be answered. An old-fashioned canvas suitcase, half full of clothes and money, lay open on a low-slung single bed. He quickly made the four steps across the small bedroom to the attached closet that was a bathroom and grabbed his wet pack. He had scooped a razor, toothbrush, paste, and soap off the cabinet top and into the small bag just as the call connected. He threw the wet pack into the suitcase, flipped over the top half, and started to zip it closed.

"*Aye?*" The voice on the phone was thin and annoyed.

Chanchai glanced out the window again. "Something is wrong. I'm being followed. What is our visibility on the woman?"

"*We are fine. No one saw us enter, and I have laid sufficient distractions for the dimwitted police.*"

"I'm not convinced. I'm going to lie low for a while."

"Do I need to remind you of your alignment?"

"It does work both ways. I have information, too. I know one person who would be particularly interested in our arrangement."

"What happened at the house?"

"Someone called the police on us. We were tapped into the radio, and the call came in before we'd even got out of the car. Some *faran* was running around, ruined the whole thing."

"There would be only a limited number of people who would know."

"Correct. I don't want to use the word traitor."

Their conversation halted as Chanchai waited for the response.

"If you're that worried, then I can only agree, as long as I have your word that you've told no one else. Where are you now?"

"At the office, packing."

Chanchai paused as footsteps passed by his door. His pistol was in the suitcase, out of reach. The footsteps faded, and he let out a long sigh.

"Do you want me to assist with anything? I shall send the money to your account."

Chanchai checked out the window one final time. Although the streets looked as normal as any night of the week, he still had a deep-seated feeling of threat. The walls of the tiny room were cramming in on him. "No. I'll take it from the safe."

"Wait until I get there."

Chanchai disconnected the call and grabbed more cash from the safe and threw it in his suitcase.

He then checked his wristwatch. It was too much of a risk waiting around. He started to dial the cell, but then hesitated. He couldn't make the call on it. He was calling the person he'd stolen it from. The number would be a giveaway. He reached for the old office phone and dialed.

"Have you lost your phone again?" Chanchai asked when

the other person answered.

"*How did you know?*" The new speaker's voice was lighter and higher than Chanchai's, although it still carried a similar menace.

"I just tried to call you, and it rang out." A quick lie to help support his plan.

"*What do you want?*"

"It's time. We need to go. Something's happened that jeopardizes everything."

"*What?*"

"It's complicated. Get your stuff ready to leave and arrange the airline tickets. I'll be in touch." He replaced the receiver.

A final sweep of the room for anything incriminating. The whole wall packed with folders was damaging, but not for him, although his scrawled entries didn't paint him in a positive light. The best solution would be to burn the place to the ground, but as each moment ticked by, he felt the heat of scrutiny bearing down. Maybe there was some value in protection. He reached out for the latest folder, but hesitated when he heard a shout from the street.

He abandoned his thought and reached for the door. He scanned the room one final time. The safe was locked. It wasn't even the most important piece in the room, but maybe it could distract anyone who came here. He gave the door handle a wipe with a thin, white cloth, then removed the gloves and stowed them in his pocket.

*

Across town, in a dark room with walls covered in pictures of Amanda, sat a silhouetted figure. He was still staring at the phone receiver, the disconnected signal beeping out of the tiny speaker. He replaced the receiver in its hook and thought for a moment. What had happened at the house? He selected another number and dialed. He whispered an address into the mouthpiece. Then the line went dead.

*

Sean gripped his pistol as people bumped into him. He stood in the center of the pavement. Busy people engaging in profits of the night crowded the street. Dealers tried harassing him until he gave them a severe glare.

The pool of his negative commerce began to grow and attract attention. Shop owners pointed at Sean as he stood still in the heart of the passing trade. The hired muscle located in the front of the stores, there to protect the less legal industries catering to tourists, examined the unknown foreigner dressed in black with a backpack. The attention moved him toward his destination.

An ancient building, bearing a stone facade weathered and worn by the environment into a patchwork of grays, lay ahead. The facing windows were small, all covered with ragged materials. A curtain flicked aside on the upper level, but no one appeared in the gap. Light emitted from only two windows. The name plaques next to the door, most written in Thai script, listed eight companies. The lower windows were barred, solid and thick steel.

A light on the lower floor went out. The metal door opened, and an old lady carrying cleaning equipment struggled outside. Sean charged for the door, but couldn't slip his fingers into the gap in time. The woman gave him an accusatory stare as she walked away.

Sean leaped after her, grabbing her arm. "*Excuse me, ma'am,*" he said, switching into Thai.

"*What?*"

"*Who works here?*"

"*I don't know.*"

"*It will be better if you tell me the truth.*"

She glared at the hand clutching her. "*Let me go or …*" Her eyes flicked over to the bouncers lining the street.

"*I need to get in. Someone inside has killed a friend.*"

"*It's nothing to do with me.*" She opened her mouth to scream.

Sean withdrew his Beretta from his pocket. "*I'd rather you didn't do that.*"

The bouncers started to move toward him. Sean glanced around, gauging the severity of the situation. Big men, probably armed with hair-trigger patience.

But the woman moved back to the door, grumbling under her breath, and unlocked it. He passed her a one-hundred-dollar US bill, which she clutched out of his hand and quickly left. The bouncers were closing in around him. Sean slipped through the door, letting it slam shut. The short corridor inside the building had two doors on either side, a potted palm at the end, and a steep stairwell ran around the corridor walls, spiraling up to the four floors above. He tried the doors on the ground floor. The left office was completely empty, with a couple of rats nibbling at something in the center of the room. The right office smelled strongly of bleach. Apparently cleaned by the old lady.

He pushed aside the excessive leaves of the plant and exposed the lift.

The lift had an old-fashioned metal grating that allowed him to see in but didn't fully enclose the elevator. He pressed the button. Old machinery creaked and groaned as the lift came down. Time was short, so he took the stairs. He ran around to the first floor, checking the offices. The doors were open. Inside was dark. The lift coasted past him to the ground floor as he took off for the upper flights. Sean heard the lift reach the lobby as he emerged on the second story landing. As he reached for the door handle, he paused. There had been someone in the lift.

He heard the grating open. Glancing over the balcony, he saw a man emerge out of the lift and walk toward the exit. Sean ran down the stairs. As he reached the first floor, the man opened the door. From the elevated height in the dim light, the profile matched that of the heavyset man he'd seen in the footage from Amanda's house. The man opened the front door, paused as he glanced over his shoulder, caught Sean's outline in the shadows, and strode outside. Sean ran down to the door, flicked the lock to its open position, and pushed out into the crowd.

The man had vanished, and now the bouncers were closing in back around Sean. Something about the man's face had triggered his memory. He'd seen him recently. In fact, earlier that day at the house.

Sean retreated into the building and flicked the lock closed. He ran up the stairs to the third floor. The office to his left would match up to the lit window. The door was locked. He pulled out his pick set and had the rudimentary lock open in seconds, revealing a small office. A small desk lamp sat in the corner. Its dim glow lit the room enough to explore without drawing too much attention.

The office was four meters square, crowding in the modest furniture and fittings. Thick ring binders, grouped into years and then alphabetically, packed one wall. He pulled out one folder from 1988. Names printed in neat handwriting in blue ink down the left, a date, then a dollar amount. Small figures. A hundred dollars. Sometimes less.

On the central desk was a decade-old monitor attached to a tower PC, probably matching in age. Sean ran his hands over the keyboard; the keys were sticky. He picked up the handset of the nearby phone. The mouthpiece smelled rank. A small safe sat below the window. The dial on the safe's front clicked around easily. The only remaining piece of furniture was a thin-legged chair in the corner. He doubted it would take his weight. A semi-concealed doorway led into another room, no more than a closet. A single bed fitted along the entirety of one wall. Filthy sheets were piled at one end. A wardrobe took up the remaining space. He slid open the wardrobe's door and peered in. It was mostly empty. Some clothes lay at the base of the unit, but the drawers were empty. He froze. On the other side of the thin walls, he heard footsteps on the creaking floorboards. He pulled out his Beretta and slipped back into the office. The door handle inched around.

07

THE DOOR OPENED, and a shadow fell in across the floor. Two quiet footsteps brought the visitor to the threshold. The door remained open as the figure hesitated in the corridor, soft breaths being brought under control. A woman entered the room. Sean leveled his pistol at her. She let out a small squeak and raised her hands. Mousey brown hair tied back. Possibly on either side of thirty. Loose clothing. Tanned. Perfect teeth. No wedding band. Small ring on right hand. No other jewelry. Healthy. Possible gym junkie. Dressed for the humidity.

"Who are you?" Sean demanded.

"I'm Lindsey," she stuttered, glancing from side to side. "What are you doing here?"

Sean waved the gun in the air. "I ask the questions. Understand?"

She nodded, her eyes filling with terror. He motioned for her to close the door and sit. Lindsey reached for the door handle and eased it closed. She shuffled over to the single chair in the corner.

"What business happens here?"

"It's, sort of, specialized transfers," she replied in staccato bursts.

"Transfers of what?"

"Money." She paused, swallowing. "From more liberal, open-market clients."

"What is your involvement?"

"I, er, keep the books."

"Bookkeeper? Why're you in so late? These are hardly business hours."

"I-if you don't mind, I'd rather not answer anything until I know a bit more about who is asking the questions. Are you the police?"

"Do I look like the police at all?" Sean indicated his black clothes, scuffed and ripped from his various chases. "Answer my questions. This place has a bedroom. Who lived here?"

"No one lived here. Sometimes business acquaintances or contractors who were traveling through wanted an out-of-the-way place to stay or do whatever with the locals."

"So why are you in so late?"

"I'm flying out tomorrow, and I wanted to get some things." Her eyes pivoted over to the small safe under the window. "I didn't want them finding out about the things I was taking."

"A bit of advice: don't ever try and take anything of theirs, even though they stole it or got it through illegal means."

"They won't miss it. They won't even know. I've balanced things so there is an unknown surplus."

"How much?"

"Fifty thousand euros."

"And they won't notice?"

"Not with the amount that passes through."

"Where are you going?"

"Rome. Italy."

"I know where Rome is."

"Sorry. American habit. Italy rather than New York."

Sean glanced over at the 1988 folders. Fifty thousand would easily and instantly be obvious in a small-time operation like this.

"You're not the usual type. How'd you get involved in this?"

"I was working at the state telephone company, and it was taking forever to save enough money. Someone asked if I'd be interested in some after-hours work for cash. Then this became a better return on my time investment."

"Why are they using such an old-fashioned system?"

"Beside my own observations of my bosses being the cheapest bastards on the planet, have you heard the phrase 'It is written'? They write it down, you can't argue. A physical record is harder to fake than a digital one, in their eyes at least."

Sean pointed over to the last folder. "Open up the latest records."

Lindsey stood and made her way over to the bottom left of the filing system. She pulled out a folder with only a few sheets clamped inside. She opened it and placed it on the desk. "So, what are you looking for?"

"I don't know yet," Sean said.

"I may be able to help. I know them pretty well."

"A friend of mine was killed by someone who came to this room in the last hour. I'd like to know his name and who he works for."

"A good friend?" Lindsey asked.

"Why are you asking?"

"This is a risk. These people are not the nicest people around."

"He was one of the extremely few people I share a secret with," Sean said. He ran his finger down the line of entries until he hit the bottom. Each was exceptionally neat and legible except for the last. Hiding in the middle of the column was an anomaly. "Who is Hydra?"

"I don't know," Lindsey said, shrugging.

"There are entries for a thousand here, two thousand there. A couple in the ten thousands. Then one figure for eight hundred and fifty thousand next to Hydra."

"Yes."

'What do you mean 'yes'?" Sean asked.

"It is unusual. It's also another reason why I want out. *That* is something big, and when a small operation goes big, you attract the attention of big police and other big illegal operations. Small is better. Stay under the radar."

"Fifty thousand is hardly under the radar."

"It's enough. I calculated that it would cost them more than that to chase the money down. You can see my working out if you want," Lindsey said.

"You may find this contradictory, but with these types of crooks, there is a principle at stake. They can't let people see them being ripped off. Otherwise others will try." Sean paused. "You mentioned sending people. That would be a contract."

The name *Chanchai* had been written as the last entry, with twenty thousand scrawled next to it.

"That's not my writing," she said.

"Maybe he filled it in himself," Sean suggested

"No one's allowed to do that."

"You've obviously never hung out with contract killers before. Otherwise, you'd know they do what the fuck they want. You've heard of 'Chanchai' before?" Sean said.

"No. Maybe I should leave a note."

Sean leafed back through the pages. Nothing came close to the Hydra figure. It was unusual. But not his concern. He had a name, albeit a first name, but something nonetheless. He tapped his fingers on the table as he combed through the figures.

Some names he knew: lowlifes and disreputable people good for squeezing out information. The problem with that, though, is most were dead. Squeezed a little too hard. *Chanchai.* Somewhere in this office there would be another name or some information attached to that one. Where would it be? Safe? Filing cabinet?

"If you don't mind me asking, you also don't look like the kind who normally comes through here," Lindsey said. She sat in the corner with her hands still raised, shifting her feet under the chair. He noticed her fidgeting.

"I do mind. Why is there a question mark next to Hydra?"

"They told me to put it there. I believe it's because it's not definite."

"It's a big figure not to be sure about. You can put your hands down."

She lowered her hands, clenching and unclenching them to get the circulation back into them. "I think you're overestimating the abilities of the operators."

Sean went silent. He moved uneasily from foot to foot. *If she is getting on a flight, where's her luggage?* The hairs on the back of his neck bristled.

"What is it?" Lindsey asked. Concern punctuated her face.

He smiled at her, without warmth, his eyes becoming unfocused. She felt a compulsive urge to smile back. The air between them became motionless and highly charged, like the molecules between them were frozen.

"You brought them here," Sean said.

The door burst open.

*

Sean dived behind the desk. Bullets pounded into the old Sonokeling, still hard despite the humidity. The gunman's silencer didn't make much difference, thanks to Lindsey's screams. The gunman turned and swung his arm around, smashing the back of his fist across her face, assisted by the weight of the pistol, knocking her to the ground. He cocked the gun and aimed at her head.

Sean tackled the gunman, using the opportunity provided by his distraction with Lindsey, and the two crashed against the shelving. The folders tumbled around them. The bullet sliced astray of Lindsey, the silencer dissipating the attack into a hushed failure. The gunman launched a volley of heavy uppercuts into Sean's stomach, until Sean grabbed a folder to defend himself. The man's hand bent against the thick file, causing him to wince. Sean brought the folder down on his attacker's head. Ducking out of the way, the gunman thrust Sean against the metal shelving, jabbing one of the steel brackets into his back. Sean cried out in pain. Having knocked Sean's gun away in the melee, the attacker brought around his own gun. Sean stepped in and blocked the man's arm as he fired two shots, sending the bullets wide.

Sean caught the man's pistol hand and smashed it against the shelving, running the back of it against the sharp undersides. The gunman's hand flinched and his pistol fell free. Sean's victory was snatched away as a brutal left hook caught him across his jaw, knocking his head against the metal. The attacker launched a series of tight punches. Sean raised his arms and parried the blows coming in from both sides, taking the pounding on his forearms. A low straight from the man landed in Sean's stomach. Sean grabbed the gunman's arm and retaliated with a solid elbow to the man's face. The man staggered back under the assault, slipping out a dagger from his jacket lining.

Sean dived for the phone and picked up the base. Lindsey lay unconscious in the corner of the room. The man feinted twice, and Sean lashed out at the phantom strikes. A thrust came in, and Sean brought the metal base of the phone into the knife's path. The blade glanced off the metal plate and continued into Sean's flesh. He winced as the knife slipped into his abdomen. He then clasped the man's wrist with his free hand and brought around the phone across the gunman's head, causing it to smash apart in his hand. The man staggered back.

Sean kicked in the man's knee and forced him to the ground. The man swung his leg around for a similar attack on Sean's knee, twisting his leg and toppling him. They tumbled together, wrestling over the knife.

Sean glanced over to the corner, and Lindsey had gone. Hopefully, she hadn't gone to get the man's friends.

He and the man wrestled on the ground, each twisting and grappling for supremacy in the tiny room. Sean rose onto a knee and threw the man against the filing cabinet. His attacker spun around and unleashed a series of combinations that sent Sean backward, defending himself from the deft movements. Sean trod and slipped on the remains of the phone. The man pressed the knife forward toward Sean's neck. The attacker pushed the knife closer. The point pricked Sean's skin. It sunk deeper, producing a trickle of blood. He pushed on as Sean's strength faded.

Then the man's eyes defocused as pottery rained down over his head. Sean twisted the knife out and down, and rammed it into the attacker's chest. The man collapsed, revealing Lindsey standing behind him, the remains of a potted plant in her hands.

"Sorry. It was the only help I could get," she mumbled.

He stared at her. "Why did you do that?"

"You did save me. He was going to shoot me."

Sean winced and held his stomach. Blood seeped from the knife wound, as well as the injury from his night in jail. They weren't bad, but both needed attention. "Don't be crazy. Run."

"You're hurt. I can't leave you," she replied.

"You're not Florence Nightingale. I can take care of this."

Sean kicked the body and a white, coiled cable tucked around the man's ear fell free. Sean reached down for the earpiece, wincing again as he bent over. The radio was still live; noise was on the line. "I've got to move."

"I'm coming with you."

"No, you're not."

"At least let me get you to a hospital."

Sean's head swum as the room spun around him. "I can't go to a hospital. I need a quiet hotel where I can take care of this injury." He slipped to his knees, but was caught by Lindsey.

"Okay. I won't say how insane that sounds, because you do look exactly like a doctor. Would you like the Hilton?"

"There's no need to take that tone. Just somewhere local, where they won't ask too many questions."

"Wait." She knelt in front of the safe, twisting the combination dial with practiced ease until the safe swung open. "We'll need cash."

"We don't have time for this," Sean hissed.

"Shit! Most of the money's gone."

"And therein lies your moral. Never trust a criminal."

Sirens rang down on the street. Sean flicked open the curtain a few inches. Four cars blocked the roadway in both directions. Police had assembled out in the street.

"I've got to go. It's best if you stay and explain yourself."

"What, with a dead body in an illegal trading office with an empty safe?"

Sean said nothing as he limped toward the door and picked up the man's pistol.

"I can't let you go like that. You need help," Lindsey said.

They made their way out onto the landing, one step at a time. The staircase was clear. Sean inserted the earpiece he'd taken from the gunman, and he led Lindsey down to the next level.

"Another one is coming." He pulled the earphone and threw it away.

A second heavyset man appeared from around the stairwell. He was on a phone and running up the stairs two at a time.

Sean pulled the trigger. Bullets sprayed over the wall, tracking along the plaster toward the man, who dived backward behind the concrete balustrade. The pistol emptied. Sean threw it away and reached for his Beretta. The man jumped up and fired several rounds back at them. Lindsey and Sean ducked for cover. Concrete showered over them from the impacts. Shouts and whistles came in from the street. Sean fired back, his Beretta's shots ringing out in the tight enclosure, hitting the man in the shoulder and chest. He tumbled away. Sean stepped after the falling body and swept up the man's gun and phone. He glanced down toward the building's entrance.

The police were ascending the stairs.

Sean and Lindsey pushed into an office and bolted the door, waiting for the footsteps to pass. The door handle rattled. A policeman pounded on the door, shouting instructions in Thai to open up. From behind the door, Sean and Lindsey heard two heavy steps followed by a solid kick that smashed open the lock. The lights flickered on.

*

The police team charged up the stairs. Omid twisted the handle of the first room. It was locked. He pounded on the thin door which reverberated under his fists.

"Open this door. It is the police," he shouted in the local dialect. No response. He took two steps back and planted his foot against the latch, smashing open the flimsy door. The lights flickered on. Inside, the room was empty. Omid shut the door and continued up with the rest of the police. The body of a heavyset thug lay on the stairs, slumped against the wall and staring up at the ceiling. Two officers were examining a tightly grouped set of bullet wounds in the center of his chest. The accuracy caused intense conversation between the team members.

Omid continued to the top story to a tiny room packed with more police.

Another body—same build, same clothes—lay on the floor, surrounded by the trashed remains of the office. The attached bedroom had avoided the destruction, but showed definite signs that someone had been living there.

Omid's phone rang. He peeked through the curtains as he answered the call. A police car barged its way through the watching crowd.

"We're on the top floor," he said to the caller. The team members prepared to depart as Omid descended the stairs.

The police car came to a stop among the throng of people. Inspector Dumo stepped out, still talking on his phone, and glanced at the assembling people. Omid emerged from the building, and Dumo disconnected his call.

"What do we have?"

Omid cleared his throat. "Two dead bodies. An empty safe. Files scattered over the floor. Evidence of a fight, but not between the two dead men. One of the kills was professional, by a trained gunman. The second, dead from a fatal stabbing. Not professional, but what you'd expect from close quarters combat."

"Well done, Omid. The gunfire should have attracted some attention. Get a team to interrogate the neighboring businesses. Come." Dumo led the young policeman up the flight of stairs, stepping around the bodies.

"Is it drug related?" Omid asked.

"I hope so," Dumo replied. "It would be a shame if this were over a late return to the library." He smiled, but no one smiled back. Dumo shrugged and let his gaze drift over the room. He spotted one policeman picking up several of the files and placing them back on the shelves. "Don't touch anything. Not until the experts get here."

Omid handed the inspector a set of plastic gloves.

Dumo checked the binders, moving between the dates until he found the most recent. Carefully, he lifted the file and placed it on the desk and opened to the last page. "The most recent pages appear to be missing." He extracted several of the files and glanced through them. "Names and amounts. But nothing to say what was being bought and sold."

"What about the names? Can't we investigate those?" Omid asked.

Dumo removed his gloves. His eyes ran around the edges of the room, following the line of the poorly made walls.

"First, we need the name of whoever occupied this office. I doubt these will be electronically transferred funds, so we can't search the bank records. I'll get Jenna to look into—"

"What is it?" Omid turned to see what had caused the inspector to halt mid-sentence.

"Can't you see it?" Dumo asked.

He stepped in closer and signaled for an officer to shine a flashlight up at the roof. The bright spotlight caught an irregular edge along the cornice. Concealed under matching paint was a thin cable poking out from behind the holding.

"There's a security camera here," Dumo said. He pulled over a chair and stepped up onto the seat, running his fingertips over the rough paint. "Has someone got a magnifying glass?" he called out over his shoulder.

The officers let out a dutiful chuckle.

"I'm serious. And a screwdriver. Omid, get on to it," Dumo ordered.

He continued to examine the molding until a policeman appeared with both items, having retrieved them from an equipment pack in one of the cars. The tiny camera lens was flush against the wood, invisible except under focused observation. He scraped away the paint surrounding the lens, revealing its tiny form, no more than a few millimeters across. Dumo drove the screwdriver in between the wall and the molding, prying it out until the wood cracked. The camera's thin wire hung down once the broken cornice was separated from the wall. He pushed the camera out from the wood and examined it from all angles. He then gave the cable a sharp tug, and it slipped out. The cable rattled within the wall, the noise running from the ceiling. With another pull, the cable came down to the filing cabinet.

At Dumo's direction, Omid rammed a crowbar into the unit and forced open the drawer. He pulled out all the files and dumped them on the ground. Leaning the unit forward, Omid found the cable trailing into the base. He examined the drawer again by tapping on the base. It sounded hollow. He levered open the lid and pulled out a small black device with a small red button on the front. Dumo peered over Omid's shoulder. Omid pressed the button and a small SD card ejected. He handed it to Dumo.

Dumo indicated the old monitor, upturned on the floor. "See if you can rig it up so we can have a look at the card."

The officers rearranged the equipment until they produced a workable setup using an officer's phone and several cobbled-together cables.

They slipped the card into a data slot and watched the footage play. The screen had been divided into quarters. The camera was tiny, and so the images were poor and condensed.

"Cameras looking into four rooms," Dumo mused.

Omid pointed to one quadrant. "That is one downstairs. I checked that room on the way up."

As officers moved through the apartment, collecting and

bagging items, placing them on the desk, Dumo and Omid continued to watch the camera footage. A grainy black-and-white image flickered in the lower left quadrant and a solid man appeared. Dumo folded his arms across his chest.

"I recognize him. Chanchai," Dumo said. "Omid, pull the details on Chanchai and see what comes up." While Omid checked with headquarters, Dumo watched Chanchai dart around the office, taking the money from the safe, disappearing into the bedroom, reappearing with a phone pressed against his ear and a small travel case in his hand.

"We have his number," Omid reported. "It's live. If he makes a call, we can track it."

"If the phone is live," Dumo suggested, "why don't you just call it? That will get us a tracking signal."

Dumo watched Chanchai finish the call then slip the phone into his jacket pocket. He did a final check of the office and exited, switching off the light. The quadrant blacked out.

"Ringing now," Omid called out as he listened to his phone.

Behind them, a phone wrapped in plastic started to ring. Dumo glanced at it before returning his attention back to the screen. "Then whose phone was he using?"

A cleaning woman appeared in the top right quadrant of the footage and wiped down the desk and chairs, then vacuumed the room before she disappeared. Immediately after, the office's quadrant flipped from black to white as the light turned on.

Dumo sighed as he saw who had come in. "Mr. O'Reilly was here as well. I believe that when I told him to stay out of trouble, he failed to grasp the concept." He gave Omid a nudge as a prompt to laugh, but the officer didn't respond.

"Would he be that stupid?"

"It is not often a man's *intellect* that drives him along a path of desperation."

Dumo and Omid watched in silence as Sean searched the

room, disappearing into the bedroom before reappearing. Then a new person entered, a woman. At lightning speed, Sean leveled his gun at her. She sat in the now-destroyed corner chair.

"Do we know who this woman is?" Dumo asked.

Omid shook his head. "Whoever she is, I doubt she realizes how much trouble she is in. Hopefully, she'll survive the night."

"A little melodramatic, Omid."

Sean and Lindsey appeared to be talking. The police watched the action unfold as the man, now the dead body on the landing, entered, then battled with Sean around the small room. Then it was over. One dead. One injured.

"Is she helping him?" Omid asked.

Then Sean and the woman were gone. The quadrant: dark.

"Check to see if anything else is on that card," Dumo said to Omid, who skipped through the remaining footage as Dumo examined the collection of evidence on the desk.

"Inspector. They're on the last bit," Omid reported.

"What?"

"Here." Omid pointed at the top left quadrant. Sean and Lindsey were standing together in another office.

"When was this recorded?"

Omid looked at the timecode. "2315. About ten minutes ago. And I checked that office when I came in."

"Lock down the building. They're still here!" Dumo roared.

Omid and the other officers charged down into the stairwell and crashed into the remaining rooms, in case Sean and the woman had moved from the previous one. Dumo ran down the stairs to the entrance and outside.

"Has anyone come out?" he shouted to the two officers he'd tasked with crowd control.

They shook their heads.

Dumo went back inside to the foyer and stared up at the ceiling. Stairs around the walls. A lift. No other exits. He turned and went back to the entrance, pausing on the threshold. Where was O'Reilly? He hadn't gotten out. The lift pinged as the doors opened. Dumo sighed and raised his hands when he then heard the familiar click of a pistol being cocked.

"Can I call you Sean, or would you prefer Simon?" he said as he slowly turned around. "We can shoot you whatever your name."

Sean smiled, his eyes cold. He had Lindsey in an arm lock with the pistol against her temple. She was shaking, terror radiating off her. "This is a modified Beretta, with an inverse trigger," Sean explained. "I press the trigger, and only when I release it, does it fire. It's a lot faster and twenty percent more accurate."

"Impressive. But pointless here."

"There is a bullet in the chamber. If my finger lets go, she dies."

"You cannot escape," Dumo said. He glanced up at the police assembling on the upper levels.

"That's not always the objective."

The police officers inched down the stairs to surround the standoff, their weapons aimed directly at Sean.

"What are you planning?" Dumo asked.

"I leave that to the professionals. I freestyle. Tell them to lower their guns," Sean demanded.

Dumo paused as his eyes flitted around the room. Only one exit and it was behind him. The sizable crowd outside would be difficult to escape through. It was impossible to tell how it would go down out in the open. Who was this man? It was obvious he believed he could survive this. The previous crime scenes where he'd seen this man kept ringing in his recollection.

Sean took a step forward. The tension ratcheted up. The foyer fell into silence. Even the crowd outside had hushed, as if sensing what was going on.

"Lower your weapons, officers," Dumo shouted. He stepped away from the exit, keeping his hands raised. "Let the woman go."

"Once I know you're not following me." Sean dragged Lindsey over to the exit.

"Then you'd better get married. What's this girl's name?"

"I didn't kill Amanda," Sean snapped.

"Come in for questioning and we can sort it out."

"I have the evidence."

"Give it to me."

"I can't. Bigger forces are at play. Once I've dealt with that you can have it. Both barrels." Sean smiled an emotionless grin.

Then he was gone. He and the nameless woman mixed into the crowd, disappearing before Dumo's eyes. He charged after them, shouting at the officers to fan out and pursue, but he knew they had vanished.

Omid charged up next to Dumo. "I'll call for support."

Dumo raised his hand. "O'Reilly runs around trying to shoot Jaide Gabat. He appears at a CIA operative's house. What interesting dots they are. Drug lord, CIA, and this place." He turned and stared back up at the office they'd been examining. "Those files are transactions, probably drugs. O'Reilly was here looking for something. Ravens. CIA. Drug money."

"Do you think we catch him?"

"Not tonight."

08

THE WHISTLES AND sirens increased in volume, coming in from all directions. With her arm around his waist, Lindsey steered Sean through tight alleyways, away from the main streets. He didn't like her tagging along; she was an unknown quantity, but for now he needed the help she was giving.

"Thank you for being believable," he said. Her body was still shaking under his grip.

"You did have a gun at my head."

"It was your idea."

"It made more sense. Added drama to the situation. Anyway, you said it wasn't loaded. Was it?"

Sean glanced at her. "I need a place a think for a few hours, where we're not vulnerable."

"I just gave up the lease on my place," Lindsey replied. "We could have gone there."

He gave her a disbelieving stare. Lindsey had said she'd wanted a life of adventure, but she was becoming psychotic about it. Her eyes were bright and alive, and she was shaking at the same time, like someone who survived a bungee jump. She looked as though she was both terrified and loving it.

"It wouldn't be safe," Sean said. "You'll be an easy thread for the police to follow, easy to track. I'll grab a cheap room. You need to get to the police and clear your name. As you said, I did have a gun pointed at your head."

"Let's get you seen to first. Then I'll go."

"No. It ends here." Sean turned Lindsey around and pushed her away into the crowd, but his blood sugar levels plummeted, and he crumpled onto one knee. Arms wrapped around his waist and pulled him up.

"Not yet," Lindsey said.

The hustle of the street buffeted them as they meandered along the narrow alleyways. Food vendors who barely occupied more room than their cookers filled the air with exotic scents and excitement. It was after midnight, and the suburb was only getting started. Sean flashed a fifty-dollar bill at a street vendor with a cabinet on wheels, which displayed a colorful row of 750ml bottles. Sean pointed at the bottle of vodka. The vendor traded it for the fifty, and Sean slipped the bottle into his pack.

"Here," Sean said as he indicated a grubby hotel, with a small, red door with peeling paint and scuff marks showing the wood underneath. The compact residence was wedged between two cheap clothing shops and was barely five meters across. The tinkling bell over the door hardly cut through the outside noise, but the old woman stationed in a back room was still able to hear it and appeared at the counter. Sean spoke to her while handing over a roll of notes, concealing his injury behind his pack. She smiled at him and Lindsey and slid a key across the counter.

They crashed in through the door to the room, and Sean collapsed onto the bed that took up three-quarters of the space. The bed was made up of two singles with separate linen. His impact shunted away the second bed, revealing a dusty and littered floor.

Lindsey fumbled with the light switch, and a sickly yellow glow dribbled out of the one central ceiling lamp. A mangled brass ring was mounted above the covered-in, thick glass bowl, full of grime and dead insects, that served as a sink. A solid, yet rusty, bolt secured an old fan to the wall. The wire frame encasing the blades was covered in dust stretching between the thin metal strands. Sean pressed the TWO setting on the fan, the big, white button clunking into place. The rattling machine hummed into life, blowing dust toward the beds.

"Better than some of the places I've backpacked in," Lindsey said after the decrepitude of the room sunk in.

"Could you turn on the telly?" Sean said as he waved toward a dusty gray box in the corner, sitting on a chair with a broken back.

"You mean the TV?"

She flicked on the old tube television. A five-button remote had been discarded on the ancient carpet. She scooped it up and threw it to Sean.

He surfed through the channels as she sat next to him on the bed examining the stab wound. "Take off your shirt."

Sean carefully peeled up the material covering the wound. Lindsey hesitated as his torso flexed in front of her, his muscles rippling as he moved.

She ran her fingers over Sean's earlier injury and its hastily applied stitches. "You've been stabbed more than once. When did that happen?"

"Last night in jail. *Not* a jail. More of a holding cell. But people like to make statements."

"You are a bad boy."

Sean pulled out the vodka and cracked the cap. Lindsey jumped up and searched the room for drinking glasses. Her expression soured as Sean poured the alcohol over the wound, wiping away the blood to examine the cut. Lindsey snatched up the bottle.

"I thought you'd got that for us. I'm still going to have a drink. Do you want one?"

Sean shook his head.

"Fine. More for me." Lindsey took a long pull from the bottle.

"We're not partners, or on a date. This is serious. You will be leaving to go to the police."

Sean reached around behind his back and removed the Beretta, placing it on the side table. She glanced at the gun.

He caught her stare. "Don't worry. I was never going to shoot you."

"Why not?"

"I only do it for the money, and there is no price on your head. You can go," he reminded her. "Just keep your head down for a few days."

Lindsey laughed. It occurred to him that the message wasn't getting through.

"What's so funny?"

"That's why I'm here." She took another sip of vodka. "I married early. I was in a difficult home situation with a step-dad who … er, wanted me to do things. I ended up getting married to the first guy who came along who could get me away. He was military. So we moved from Canada down into Ohio. It turned out he wasn't that nice, either. He wanted me to do things as well. I got really unhappy. Here, I got a photo." She flicked through her purse and held up a faded photograph.

Sean smiled. "At least you've got nice hair."

"Nice hair can't save your self-confidence when you've gained a hundred pounds. I got trapped, couldn't do anything or go anywhere, so I ate."

"Did you eat your husband?"

She laughed again. "Not really. His friend was kinda decent. He used to chat with me and we got a bit closer. Then one day, I don't know what happened, but I … er … had my head down, when my husband"—she raised the photo again—"came in and caught us. He kicked me out. I'd done nothing with my life, ever—nothing at home, nothing while locked away in a military base. So I packed a backpack and started traveling. Walking ten hours a day sure takes off the excess pounds."

Sean's smile widened. "It was certainly his loss. You're a cracker now."

Lindsey frowned. "A what?"

"A looker." He shrugged. "Hot."

Lindsey smiled back. "I promised never to be like that again. I was going to live my life for me." She toasted herself and downed more of the vodka. "I went looking for adventure. Tonight is definitely the high point."

"Adventure can be overrated. Take it from me."

She moved into the tiny bathroom and called out, "Well, what about you?"

102

"What?"

"We've been getting all deep and meaningful, and you haven't said anything about yourself."

"There's nothing to say."

She emerged with a thin hand towel, rolled it up, and stuck it in the end of the vodka bottle before upending it and soaking the material. "Oh, come on. I've told you my life story. You can give me something. Are you a spy?"

*

Henderson reeled back from her boss's verbal onslaught. Her nails dug into the soft leather of the armchair. "It's not as bad as that."

Banks waved Sean O'Reilly's file at her. "The guy's a CIA disaster area. He caused nothing but trouble during the four years he was with us. These records are a joke. What on earth made us pick him?"

"Okay, let's calm down and breathe easy on this. Have you processed the complete file? First up, ten years of exceptional service in the French Foreign Legion, working his way up to captain in some of the most desperate and hostile regions in the world."

"What did he do before that?"

"Do you know how the Foreign Legion works? The whole point is you leave your past behind. A new name, a new future."

"But ten years? Isn't the minimum term in the Legion twenty?"

"We have an agreement with them in some circumstances when certain individuals come to our attention, and we think that they can benefit us in a particular situation at that particular time."

"And they allow this?"

Henderson hesitated before answering. "As I said, there is

a protocol where exchanges can be … agreed. We have an arrangement. Usually high-level stuff. We don't get involved in each other's details. O'Reilly came to us with an exemplary record. Second-to-none covert skills. And one tough bastard. Apart from what the reports say, which is for people just like you to thrust at the media, the results have been exactly what we wanted. He's taken a lot of dirt for us over the years so we can achieve mission aims."

"So, what the hell happened? Why is he no longer part of the picture?"

"He and his team went out on a severance mission, chasing after a cell in Abbottabad in 2011."

"The OBL mission? That's a coincidence, right?" Banks said.

"This isn't my area, and it was before my time. You'll need Tom for the full breakdown. But as I said, some things happen so some other things can happen. Missions intertwine. My paperwork says the team was compromised, and two men were caught by the cell."

"I assume O'Reilly was one."

"Yeah, and Tank was the other," Henderson said. "Brad was also on the mission, but he managed to evade capture."

"We do not have someone on the books named 'Tank.'"

"Obviously not with that name. Andy McCray: hand-to-hand combat specialist. Nerves and fists of steel. He's been integral in a dozen high-profile operations."

Banks wrote the name down on a piece of paper. He tapped the pen's retractor button, lost in thought, as he stared at the name. "O'Reilly, Camden, and McCray. Where is McCray now?"

"I don't know. It doesn't really seem important with the current situation." She didn't bother to hide her frustration.

Banks leaned back in his chair and peered over the top of his glasses. "As Tom isn't around, I'm instructing you to gather the information."

"What about the fertilizer factory?"

"Leave that with me."

"I'd like to look into it. I've got a feeling something isn't adding up."

Banks paused before leaning forward on his desk. "No, check into O'Reilly and see why he went bad. You're from IA originally?"

"Yes."

"I can see the attraction of the factory, but as you said, missions intertwine. The more you understand about *existing* operations, the more valuable you are. Do you understand me?"

Henderson hesitated before nodding.

"Tread carefully," Banks cautioned. "Things are done differently in Operations."

*

"No, I'm not a spy," Sean replied.

"Go on. We'll probably never meet after tomorrow," Lindsey prompted.

He looked into her big, blue eyes, full of earnest innocence, dying for a moment of exhilaration in a life doused in drudgery. And he shrugged. "I can tell you some things."

"What about your family?"

He closed his eyes and flinched as she dabbed a vodka-soaked cloth against the wound.

"Do you need a drink?" she asked.

His eyes snapped open. "No." He swallowed. "All right. I have a mother and a younger brother."

She sipped again at the bottle. "Are they in Ireland?"

He paused. "Some are."

"Are you sure?"

"I don't like people knowing. My brother is there, but me

ma had to go. They've been threatened in the past, and I don't want that to ever happen again."

Sean reached over to his pack and pulled out a bandage. Lindsey ripped it open between her teeth and strapped it across the knife wound. She patted down the edges, securing it in place. Sean examined it and gave her a nod of approval.

"Where'd you learn first aid?"

"I lived on a military base. For several years. You're *forever* doing first aid courses." She took another swig of vodka. "You can't go back to Ireland?"

He shook his head. "Better not to. Something happened a long time ago, something I caused, and me ma's been living with the consequences of it for the last … nearly twenty years. And because of that, my brother is in jail. Stupid kid should never have gone. He wasn't built for it, mentally or physically."

"What about your father?"

"The drunken fucker, beating up the family, stealing money, and gambling or drinking it away. Between him and me, our Rory never had a chance. How do you know what to do when your male role models are just a bunch of dumb fuckers who can't do anything right except be losers? I failed him and me ma big time."

"Can't you make it up to them?"

"Not really. I can't talk to Ma. Dangerous people are out looking for me, so she is an obvious target to watch."

"Who's looking for you?" Lindsey asked.

"People. Not nice ones," Sean replied.

"How did you get caught up with these people?"

"I won't say."

"So where do you work now?"

"Same again."

"Anything else?"

"No."

"Are you married?" she asked. She gave him a half smile.

"No comment."

"Gay?"

"No."

"You are *no* fun. If you won't talk about yourself, what about your friend, the one you went to the office about?"

Sean laughed. "Sometimes in this line of work you wonder if you know anyone at all."

Lindsey yawned, rolled onto her back, and stared up at the ceiling. The humidity of the day permeated the air, with the smell of the crowd lingering. "Is there anything you can talk about? And if the answer is sports, I *will* steal your gun and shoot you."

"Maybe I should leave it there," Sean replied. "Talk about yourself. Something tells me you're good at that."

"I am a recent fan of vodka." She closed her eyes and sighed. Sean glanced over; she appeared to have drifted off to sleep. He flicked through the TV channels looking for news programs. None of the majors were mentioning the incident, which was odd. He'd thought gunshots in a high-profile location would certainly garner attention. He flicked over to a local channel televising a Muay Thai match; two guys beating the crap out of each other. The round ended, and the program paused for a news break.

"Jesus."

"What?" Lindsey sat up to see what Sean was watching. Her face was on TV. Next to Sean's. "They have both our faces."

"And names," Sean commented.

"It says I'm wanted for questioning regarding the shooting. Shit, that's bad."

"Not as bad as being wanted for murder." Below his image a ticker tape ran with many words he'd prefer to be associated elsewhere. Murder. Suspect. Armed. Dangerous. He sighed. It seemed a little unfair. Aye, he was all those things, but not here. All the extreme efforts he had expended in keeping off the radar had all been blown in a few hours. And all because of the agency. If Tom hadn't turned up to tell him about Brad ... Their times together, good and bad, drifted through his memory. It was all about Brad and Amanda and getting those who cut their lives short. He was doing this for his friend. That was the perspective he needed to maintain. Keep the fire burning.

The information would be transmitting around the world. He'd have to hope Brad's family wasn't watching.

This wasn't being reported on the major stations, just some cheap local fleapit of a broadcaster, arguably less corrupt than some of the pay-to-play stations back in the US. He checked back on the other channels. No changes. This was Dumo at work. *What was he playing at?*

"Go and help them with their inquiries," Sean urged. "I know how they operate, and it'll be for the best."

She sat rubbing her eyes, leaning forward on her knees. "How did they find my name? I wasn't on the books. No one knew I was doing that job."

"The police are generally good at finding things out."

"Not where I'm from. They're *generally* good at eating donuts. I do not feel comfortable surrendering." She paused and looked into Sean's eyes. Her face changed, becoming determined. "I came looking for adventure."

"I wish you'd stop saying that. There is a difference."

"Do we need to go?"

"No. The lady downstairs has been paid enough. She won't want to lose her *black spot* reputation and all future customers." He pulled out the paper with the phone number he'd gotten from Hans. "How do I get info on who an anonymous call came from?"

"A major phone company would have the technology to do

it." Lindsey yawned again.

Sean glanced at his wristwatch. "Jesus. It's almost one. I'm not talking 'til morning. Let's get some rest." He turned off the light, and listened to the buzzing and pulsing streets. The chaotic life with its express business practices churned the people through the area. Anyone who'd seen them would be gone by now, hustling or sightseeing elsewhere.

He watched Lindsey succumb to exhaustion, her face relaxing as she drifted into sleep.

She was awoken by the quiet click of the door as it opened.

*

Henderson clapped her hands as she entered the logistics room, startling the team into attention. She paced in front of the matrix of displays, with the heads turning to follow her.

"What was Sean O'Reilly's last mission?"

"Last listed mission was 2011, Abbottabad," an analyst called out.

"Good. Pull up everything we've got on Andy McCray and Sean O'Reilly. McCray was there, too. He had to file a report. I need an infodump, especially between the two, and throw it up on the screens. Any questions, any abnormalities—no matter how small—fire them at me."

Henderson stepped back at the end of the front row facing the monitors, but without focusing on them. She tapped her fingers on the desk beside her, and stared at the floor. Banks was hiding something. After all the years in IA, she could smell his deception.

Palmer gave her a quizzical look. "You appear distracted," the linguistics expert said.

Henderson sat down and leaned in toward her and lowered her voice. "Why is Banks leading us away from the Russian problem? Verity, do a search on it. See if anything cross-correlates."

"With what? I have to have a set of parameters to run a model."

Henderson sighed. "Do we have access to black ops data?"

"No."

"Pull up the data on the location, but not on the big screen. Just your monitor. Let's see if we can reverse-engineer something."

Palmer's fingers danced over the keys and information zipped across the screen. Henderson squinted and reached for her glasses. "Show me a satellite feed. Zoom in."

"I can't, not without the feed appearing on the screens," Palmer replied.

Henderson glanced around before standing up. "Okay people, change of objective. Go back to Prigorodny. Someone get me a satellite feed."

A grainy image appeared on the central screens. "Magnification height about fifty yards," someone called out.

"Is that maximum?" Henderson said.

"Yes, ma'am. It's the best we have authorization for."

"Authorization?"

"We are loaning a Chinese satellite," the analyst reported. "None of ours will be over the area for hours. It'll be dark by then."

Henderson's face reddened and she raised her voice. "People, this is poor work. We have to do better." She pointed at the screen. "This is the image, and it's the best we're going to get. What can we determine? I want you thinking hard about this."

"There's a truck."

"Is there a logo on the side?" Henderson asked.

"I can't make it out."

"What about color? Is grainy black and white the best we can do? Is there some way of capturing the image then decoding

110

it later when the satellite is over the site? Or can we color match with existing sat pictures of the area?"

"I'm working on it," another analyst called out.

"Okay, let's keep the momentum," Henderson said. "Let's examine the site. What can we see?"

"Three targets blown. Place looks a bit of a mess," a young man called out.

"It certainly doesn't look like a fertilizer factory. Do we have any tactical experts here?"

The young man raised his hand.

"Name?" Henderson asked.

"Daniel Price."

"Okay, Daniel Price, explain." She waved him down the front.

He jumped up and came up to the screens, pointing at the sites around the facility.

"These are detonations," he said, pointing out black smears over the ground. "It means it was a professional hit. This mark is out of proportion with the others, bigger, meaning it has detonated something more explosive."

"Like fertilizer?"

"Yes. If it was ammonium nitrate. Depending on how much was stored there, it could demolish the plant."

"But say it was fertilizer, why are there other marks?" She pointed at the other locations.

"Tactically, these would be decoys. Except ... why so many? Normally, you'd have one or two, but here we have four."

"And that means?"

"Multiple targets," Price said. "If you have a real fertilizer factory explosion, like Waco in 2013, then it's a mess. This is focused and controlled."

"And if trucks are still going in and out?" Henderson asked.

"It's still operating. Normally, a fertilizer factory blows up and it's shut down. Health and safety. Excavation of dead. That kind of thing. This is still operating. Its customers are people who cannot wait."

"So, it's not a fertilizer factory, and we have evidence that we had a team out there who probably blew it up. Yet, we have no records."

Banks entered the operation room, focusing on the folder in his hands. "Henderson, I'm going through the O'Reilly case file …" He paused as he took in the scene and the image on the display. The room quietened. "What are you doing?"

"I'm correlating information between McCray and O'Reilly," Henderson said

"That is the factory."

"Yes, the clearest link we have between them is with Brad Camden."

"That's a load of crap. I told you to keep away from this," Banks said.

"But they are linked."

"And your evidence is what exactly?"

Henderson sighed. "We're working on it."

"Not anymore. Shut it down. Come with me."

09

THE LOGISTICS ROOM sat idle with the team members talking to one another in lowered voices. The minute hand crawled around the clock face. Forty-five minutes later, Henderson returned. Her shoulders were sagging and her head bowed down. People sat still as she moved to the front, standing in between the team and the oversized monitors, now blank. She cleared her throat.

"Sean O'Reilly. We got him from the French Foreign Legion. Palmer, pull up our information on the recruitment."

Palmer rattled off several French sentences. Henderson stared at her. "Sorry. I was confirming your command," Palmer said. "I was in the Paris office for six years before coming here."

"Of course, you're linguistics. Good accent by the way. Post up the 2011 Abbottabad mission. Andy McCray. Please tell me it's not still encrypted by the eye."

"Clear," Price called. "It's an archived record."

"Thank God for that. Something is finally going our way. Feed me."

"What are we looking for? Can you be a bit more descriptive?"

"O'Reilly, McCray, and Camden all worked together on that mission. It was their last one together. There must have been reports."

"What about the level one mission in Thailand?" Price asked.

"Banks says he'd sort something out." She pulled out her phone and checked the time. "See if his authorization has come through."

Price typed quickly. "Yes," he said. "Well, sort of. The eye was Beck Williams. And that is it. Nothing else has been cleared."

"Great." Henderson muttered.

"You know Williams?" Palmer asked.

"I know she's a hard ass. I've had to deal with her before. She'll throw up every barrier to keep her authority unquestioned. Let's see if Banks can get any further with his clearance request. Anyway, focus on Abbottabad."

The team members brought up the data. Electronic documents filled the monitors.

"It's listed in the records as a standard raid, searching for a weapons depository," Palmer said.

"Then why did we publicize it as an attempted cell corruption?" Henderson asked. "Was there a cell there or not?

We have pictures of captured soldiers. I don't get it. We sent in a task force to rescue them. Why did we send them looking for weapons in a place we were fairly certain OBL was located?"

Price raised his hand. "I'm getting the reports for Abbottabad."

"Have you got McCray's report?"

"Ah ... sort of." Price said. "The heading is here. But the actual report has been redacted."

"By *who*?"

"Looks like Williams."

Henderson groaned. "What was the reason?"

Price paused as he read the note aloud. "McCray's mental stability was unreliable. He was plagued by delusional episodes and PTSD."

"McCray ... where is he? Anyone?"

"Last known location is"—Palmer checked her screen—"classified."

"You have got to be kidding me. The one man who can provide some clarification on the situation is uncontactable. Can this get any more difficult?" Henderson paced the room. "How about Camden? Did he write anything?"

"No, too junior."

"I know Brad Camden, I shared drinks with him last Christmas. He was outspoken about a lot of things. I find it hard to believe he had nothing to say on the mission. O'Reilly was his friend, a mentor, who betrayed the team but saved him. That had to resonate on some level. Did he have private notes? Did he visit psych?" She turned to Palmer, who was concentrating on her screen. "Verity, did you hear that? Could you scan his e-mail?"

Palmer nodded. Henderson turned back to Price.

"Okay, back to O'Reilly. What did Williams's report say?"

"The bullet points are"—He raised a finger—"one, sent in

team to find weapons."

"I'm calling bullshit on that. Williams knew it wasn't."

Price read ahead. "Two, someone tipped off al-Qaeda that the team was coming. So, that's how they got captured."

"Someone called the al-Qaeda? And what, left a voice mail?"

"Yes," Price confirmed.

"Sorry? Explain that."

"Information was relayed to them that there would be a strike. They were waiting. Two men got captured, O'Reilly and Tank ... McCray. The others managed to escape."

"How is that possible?"

"You're not going to like this. There is a private note from Williams on the file. She claimed that O'Reilly was the source of the leak and told al-Qaeda he was coming."

"Why?"

"The bad case scenario is so he wouldn't get tortured."

"Was he?"

"Not according to the reports."

"So, O'Reilly was"—Henderson scanned the team—"what? Working with al-Qaeda? Then how did we ... This is getting ridiculous. I'm going to speak with Banks. Again."

Ireland
Location: Dundonald House (State Prison)
Year: 1994

The cold of the Irish winter sunk through the grey, stone walls. Rasping breaths and coughs of the prisoners punctuated the silence. U2's recent hit, "Lemon," played on a tinny transistor radio. Sean fought through the grogginess. Someone asked him a question. Images floated in and out of focus, growing large before diminishing. He could hear other voices, but this one was close, the voice of the man who'd saved him. The smell of cleaning agents cut through the air, providing the only definite sensation. Sean rolled his head to the side. The man's huge face, concealed behind a thick beard, loomed over him. A ham-sized fist, its knuckles lined with scars and fresh scabs, rested on Sean's chest.

"Well, Sean, I'm Joseph Savage—they call me Big Joe, and as you may tell from my delicate knuckles, I run the ring in the yard."

A massive hand waved in Sean's face. It came to rest again on his chest and tapped against his ribcage, causing him to wince.

"I've never seen someone survive such a beating from the Proddies." Joseph laughed. "But, you're in danger now. That bit o' defiance'll make 'em angrier, and in here there's limited protection. My advice to you is to prepare. You're a big lad. Come down to the ring and learn how to handle yourself. Get some respect. You'll never be a daddy, but at least you won't be at the other end." He paused. "And never tell the bastards who you are."

"Why?" Sean asked.

"You got family on the outside?"

"I see."

*

As soon as he could stand, Sean had been given a cell next to Joseph. People stayed away, and the boredom of isolation settled in.

Each day a short, elderly prisoner came by and followed the same ritual: Pause outside the door. Look both ways. Step inside into the corner of the room. Light half a rollup that disappeared with a couple of deep inhalations. Ask the question.

"Cannae ya move without bleeding?"

Within a fortnight, Sean confirmed his recovery. The old man smiled.

"Then ya with me." He bowed and slipped into a fake British accent. "Big Joe requests your attendance."

The old man led Sean down the steel walkways and staircases. The rest of the prisoners were in the mess for lunch and the facility was quiet. Sean shivered as soon as he hit the outside air of the exercise yard. Several guards and prisoners who visited Joseph regularly had formed a cordon, surrounding Big Joe. His breath billowed out in the freezing air. The compound's whitewashed walls, barely thick enough to cover the blocks, towered above, allowing a glimpse of the eternally gray sky. An indifferent painter had plastered a navy border around the base of the wall, often spilling over to the rough concrete floor. It was mid-winter, and Sean was dressed in a T-shirt and a set of old shorts, both so worn and dirty they had taken on a new color and texture more akin to soil than material.

"You ever boxed?" Joseph asked.

"No," Sean replied through chattering teeth.

"You do now. Tie on a pair o' eights."

Joseph pointed over at a sad collection of abused equipment. Sean fumbled, struggling to slip his hands in the tight straps of the eight-ounce gloves.

"You're meant to loosen them a wee bit first," one of the guards muttered.

Joseph stepped into the ring, ducking between the ropes. He towered a foot above Sean, his bare arms as thick as Sean's legs.

"Come on, boy. Let's see what you got. Put your hands up to protect your head," he said.

Sean raised his gloves to either side of his face. Joseph smirked, stepped in and smacked Sean's glove, which swung in and bounced off his face.

"Keep the gloves close otherwise you end up punching yourself. Like this." Joseph demonstrated the correct stance.

Sean moved around, stepping from side to side. Joseph watched him like a predator inspecting its prey. Sean swung wildly. Joseph sidestepped him and landed a blow on the back of Sean's head, sending him sprawling to the ground. Fury brewed within Sean. He leaped up and threw a flurry of blows at Joseph, who reeled back under the surprise attack. Joseph slipped in a straight punch then sent a right cross through the gap, landing the punch squarely on Sean's jaw.

"You need to control your anger," Joseph warned. "Best advice I ever received. It'll be the best you get, too. What brought you in here?"

"An accident."

Joseph let Sean land a couple of blows against his own gloves. They were solid, and Sean showed good extension. "Your records said manslaughter."

"How did you read …?"

"I always liked that word. *Manslaughter*. Sounds better than murder. You slaughtered a man."

"It doesn't mean that. And I didn't," Sean protested.

"None o' us did." Joseph gave him a smile. "We're all innocent, just victims o' circumstance. So, who was it? Someone after your girl?"

"No. My brother clashed with a Proddies rally." Left. Left. Right hook. "We'd been drinking."

"You're a bit young to be drinking."

"It was a brawl." Right hook—miss. "I didn't even realize what was happening. They outnumbered him and were giving him a right seeing-to. I was so out of it I didn't know what I was doing." Right hook, left hook, right hook. No impact. "I was smashing this guy in the face"—right hook, left hook, uppercut—"and they said they had to drag me off him. Said I had a psychotic episode." Sean unleased a series of hooks until he ran out of breath, all of which broke against Joseph's guard. "He died later from head injuries." Sean lowered his gloves and stared at his shoes.

"Maybe best if you lay off the laughing juice. Try a combination."

Left. Right. Wide right hook. The blow slipped through Joseph's defense, him half-dropping his guard. Sean's punch knocked into his jaw, but Joseph remained unrattled.

"You are a fast bastard, no mistake," Big Joe complimented. "But you need more strength. Let's get some meat on those bones. I'll have a talk with the warden. He takes care o' his thoroughbreds."

Joseph stood still, lowered his left glove and drove a high punch with his right straight through Sean's defenses that landed him on the concrete. Big Joe threw a towel on top of the sprawled boy. "Take him back."

The guards gathered around Sean, lifted him onto his feet, and hustled him back to the cell.

The resonance of the slamming door filled Sean with a loneliness. Each time it was shut, he'd sit on the pile of rags on a bug-infested mat masquerading as his bed, and place his head in his hands. The pounding from Joseph had rattled him and stars spun across his vision. In the anonymous white-washed walls, Sean faced the truth. For people like him, the place wasn't a prison, it was a morgue.

*

The guards reappeared some time later and dragged Sean to the governor's office, where Joseph was already waiting. The governor sat behind a large desk and reclined in a towering leather chair, resplendent in his sharp, shiny gray suit. He didn't speak, but listened to Joseph's enthusiastic descriptions.

The governor smiled and nodded.

Things changed immediately. Each morning before the sun rose, a guard dragged Sean from his bed amid the snores and murmurs to the mess, where he was fed an egg-heavy breakfast. He felt odd, lonely, sitting by himself in the mess, watched by three guards. But the cooked breakfast was better than the gruel the chef served to the rest of the prisoners, and an improvement over anything his poor mother had been able to concoct from meager government handouts.

Sean's frame began to fill out, and his body began to sculpt into that of a lean athlete. Training took place every morning and afternoon, with the governor occasionally dropping by to see how Sean was progressing.

After two months, the governor pulled Joseph aside as he watched Sean's skip rope sprints, which filled the compound with a lawnmower-speed buzz.

As he had in his office when this had started, the governor smiled and nodded.

After the governor had left, Joseph called Sean over. "Time for a tryout. Nothing major. Just a warmup. The guv wants to see how his investment is going before he decides whether he wants to continue."

"What if I lose?" Sean asked.

He patted Sean solidly on the shoulder and gave him a stern stare. "Let's not make that an option."

*

Twenty-four hours later, the match had been set.

Sean stood naked in the men's showers with his usual rags kicked into the corner. The noise of the waiting crowd bounced down the concrete tunnel and around the shower room. Occasional chants welled up out of the noise. He traced his finger over the embossed government crest stitched on the front of the colored shorts. Orange. Purple. Green. The prison drove all style out of you, but still the colors clashed. Everything, everywhere had some green splash. A madness gripping an entire people. Patriotic to the last drop of blood.

"You worried?" Joseph asked.

"No," Sean replied.

"Get dressed. They'll talk if you go out like that."

Sean pulled on the silk shorts. He sat and tied on his shoes. A bench screeched as Joseph pulled it over the tiles. He sat opposite Sean and wrapped his hands in tape.

"Why are we fighting?" Sean asked.

"Besides for profit and respect? It's a part of the human psyche."

"No. Us. The Irish."

Joseph shrugged as he slipped the gloves onto Sean's hands. "Blame the drink."

"I can't keep doing that."

"Simple. Don't drink. It got you in here. This," he said, knocking the gloves, "will get you out. Your mate waiting out there is a Proddy. One o' them bastards that gave you a seeing-to. You want to be better than this? You want to send them a message? Now is the time."

Joseph held out his fists. Sean tapped his own against the wall of fingers.

The sweating maintenance staff tied off the last of the canvas tensioners as Sean emerged from the showers. No one cheered. A banner matching the clashing colors of his shorts had been suspended from the walkway around the top of the compound. Joseph pulled the ropes apart and Sean clambered up into his corner. The inmates were focused on Sean's opponent, cheering as he raised a fist to them. He was big and covered in victory tattoos. This was his home and he wasn't in a hurry to get out. Joseph lifted himself up into the ring and checked

Sean's gloves a final time.

The bell rang.

Joseph slapped Sean on his back and stepped out. "Remember what they did."

The fighters moved into the center of the ring and circled. They stood eye to eye, with Sean's opponent visibly wider at the shoulders. Sean bounced from foot to foot and let his opponent's early attacks thump against his gloves. The punches had weight. The man muttered something, but the words were lost in the cries from the crowd.

The world ebbed away from Sean, leaving only the man in front of him, a giant ghost against the darkness. His breathing slowed and his heartbeat thumped in time with his movements. The moment slowed and the shouts faded into echoes. The man's shoulders twitched, telegraphing his attacks. Sean ducked under the swings. Rising on the outside, he drove his left fist over his opponent's extended arm and into his jaw. The moment dissolved as the crowd went silent.

His opponent fell to the ground. It had taken seven seconds.

Blood sprayed over the canvas in a long streak as his head bounced against the canvas. The medical staff flooded in and surrounded the fallen man. Sean paced around the remaining half of the ring, largely ignored.

In the corner of the room, the governor pulled Joseph aside, and again smiled and nodded.

*

Sean was relocated to a "convenient" cell for his training. It seemed farther away to him, but it was secluded and nowhere near the Proddies.

His first training partner was a towering man with a bald head, cauliflower ears, and bloodied knuckles. When he smiled, it revealed several gaps. His arms were tree trunks, and he was fast as a striking snake, with moves as dirty as a dancer.

But Sean, to Joseph's astonishment, was faster, and he began to read the great thug's moves before he made them. Each week, Sean would get a new opponent, and each was dispatched in record time.

Even fighters from regional prisons came. Then they left, with head back and nose pinched to stop the blood.

One morning the tall, bald man came to fetch him. He wrestled Sean away in a headlock until they reached the Proddy section of the cellblock, where the bald man gave a nod to the guard, who unlocked the gate so Sean could be flung into the compound.

Some had been told the Mick was coming and word spread. This time, no gloves and all the dirty blows a dozen men could throw.

It was never going to be an even fight, and Sean did take some crippling blows. But not before he'd made a mess of many of the Proddies.

And the governor smiled and nodded when he heard.

The guards had rushed in, whistles blasting, thrashing their batons. Someone had to protect the Proddies. Joseph carried Sean out, but on his shoulders. Black and blue and covered in dozens of scratches and cuts, no one had taken Sean down.

And the man standing next to the governor, who looked like an accountant, smiled and nodded too, and handed over a thick brown envelope before he turned and left.

Late the next night, Sean awoke as his bunk shook. He rubbed his eyes as Joseph's bearded smile came into focus.

"How did you get in? Christ, I might as well install a revolving door," Sean grumbled.

Joseph shushed him, after clipping him around the ear for taking the Lord's name in vain, and signaled for Sean to follow. Sean rose and stepped down onto the cold concrete floor. His body still ached from the fight. They headed away from the compound, away from the canteen, away from the Proddies, and toward the front gate. Joseph faced Sean and shook his hand, then hugged him in his great bear arms.

"We've taken you as far as we can. Someone is interested in your skills."

*

Thailand
Location: Bangkok
Time: 0249

"Where have you been?" Lindsey hissed.

Sean raised two passes as he pushed his way back into the small hotel room. "I didn't want to wake you. I obtained some cleaner passes for TOT, then got our photographs on them."

He dropped them onto the table before lying down on the other single bed and closing his eyes.

She picked up the pass and examined it. "Where did you get the photo of me?"

"Oh yeah," he said as he withdrew her passport from his back pocket. Without opening his eyes, he threw it across the gap between the beds. It landed in her lap.

"How did you get this? It was in a *very* private place."

"Yeah, it was."

Lindsey blushed as Sean turned off his bedside lamp. The early morning sounds drifted in through the window, and the temperature and humidity had retreated, allowing Sean and Lindsey to drift off into sleep.

As the morning sun crept in through the window, Sean awoke and examined his wounds. Lindsey yawned and stretched as she awoke. The tacky plastic kettle began to steam. She glanced over at his pistol still resting on the side table by his bed.

"You don't need to come on this next leg," Sean said. "You've done enough for me, and you're already in too much trouble for a civilian."

"Life is an adventure," she replied.

"I don't think you should take that as a mantra. It'll catch up with you."

"You'll need me to get into the TOT. I know the layout of the place," Lindsey insisted.

"It's up to you."

"Can I get cleaned up? I'll be quick."

"I'm not sure if the water will actually clean you."

She disappeared into the bathroom. Running water echoed through the thin walls. Sean checked his Beretta, then glanced out through the window. A handful of merchants milled around on the quiet streets, filling in the hours before the tourists arrived. They talked in relaxed phrases that mimicked their actions. Unhurried economics.

Sean fastened his pack and placed it by the door. The water still ran. It had been good to have company for the night, and she'd been fun, but he needed to move on. It had been a bad idea to get her a pass. The water stopped. He scooped up his pack and placed his hand on the door handle. A floorboard creaked. Was it outside or in?

Behind him, Lindsey emerged out of the bathroom with wet hair, wearing her bra and jeans. The room's door handle turned under his grip.

Sean snatched open the door and came face-to-face with the barrel of a pistol. The owner of the weapon was looking down the corridor, caught off guard. Before the man could blink, Sean dropped. The man fired, the bullet skimming over Sean as he twisted out of the way. In one movement, Sean pulled out his Beretta out of his belt and fired twice. The bullet pierced through the man's head, splattering his brain matter over the far wall. Sean rolled out into the hall and fired at another man who had appeared on the floor landing. Two more shots and he fell. Sean signaled for Lindsey to follow. She grabbed her things, pulled on her clothes, and peered into the corridor.

"What were they doing there?" Lindsey asked.

"The old lady must have reported us."

"You said she wouldn't do that."

Sean shrugged, keeping his eyes on the stairwell. Lindsey pulled on her shoes, half hopping down the narrow corridor.

They climbed down the stairs. The old lady sat behind the counter, staring at the exit, a bullet in between her eyes.

"Probably not the payment she was expecting," Sean said as they crept past her.

"Should we call the police?"

"Someone would have heard the shots. They'll be on their way."

Sean slung his pack over his shoulder. He hot-wired a scooter, and the two set off across town to the TOT corporate office. Lindsey hung on to him with her hands around his waist.

*

"Jesus, why don't you install a bed in here?" Banks snarled. His face did not hide his annoyance.

"This is becoming a nightmare," Henderson said as she sat down. She found her formal and respectful demeanor in front of Banks slipping in proportion to his help. Despite the hour, he demanded answers to questions that she found to be blocked at every turn.

"How is Thailand going?" he pressed.

"We've got the eye detail on the Thai mission. It's Beck Williams."

"Typical." Banks watched the afternoon sun pour down on the park opposite the office. "Out enjoying this."

"What?"

"Williams is on long-service leave."

Henderson paused as she screamed in her head. "Do we know where? We must have an emergency contact for her."

"Don't we have the code she used?"

"That would defeat the purpose. The eye sets the code, just as Robinson is in hiding with the code over the fertilizer factory incident."

"We're the bloody CIA," Banks growled. "We're meant to be experts at cracking codes."

"We're—"

Banks leveled a finger at her. "If you're about to say, 'We're working on it,' the immediate future will not go well for you."

"… progressing." Henderson gave him a winning smile.

"Speak with admin, then."

"Williams was also the eye on the Abbottabad mission."

"The O'Reilly mess?"

"Yes. His time with us is complicated. We're taking Abbottabad as the point where he turned rogue. But the reports I found, as I read them, are contradictory."

"Didn't IA pick up on that in the audit?"

"It would appear not." Henderson became acutely aware, as the former head of IA, that if this went sideways, they'd point the finger at her. "But we'll get to the bottom of it."

"Wait, how is it contradictory?"

"Williams said it was a weapons search. Possible WMD."

"So?"

"We all know it was about OBL."

"Four years ago she was being audited," Banks said.

"The only people who should be afraid of an audit are those with something to hide," Henderson reminded him.

"Spoken like a true auditor. Let me tell you that the word alone can get people sweating."

"Okay, let's say that it was always about the weapons. Williams says O'Reilly forewarned the al-Qaeda cell that they were coming. The team turns up, and O'Reilly and McCray are captured. McCray is tortured. O'Reilly isn't. We assume because he let them know they were coming, so they could hide the weapons or something."

"So O'Reilly is working for al-Qaeda?"

"But we got OBL's location out of it." She threw her hands in the air. "To me, you don't let the enemy know you are coming then get the most valuable information they have out of them."

"But we sent men in to get them out. Couldn't that have been an unexpected response on our behalf?"

"No, I don't think it was O'Reilly who called."

Banks' face flushed. "Who then?"

"Now when we say caught by the cell, we could argue over the clarity of definition whether 'caught' is the same as allowing them to be caught. Setting it up, so to speak."

"We'd never do something like that. Our own men." Banks shook his head. "The implication that you'd think that we *would* will need to be noted. You are, in fact, calling one of our most successful and senior eyes a liar."

Henderson found it interesting that Banks leaped to defend Williams even though she clearly hadn't been named. "I am searching for information that will clarify her position on this. That's all."

"I suggest you find it quickly. What did Mr. McCray say?"

"Williams redacted his report for being an unreliable account. She questioned him as an operative. PTSD. Apparently, his torture was extreme."

"Poor bastard. And O'Reilly sold him out so he'd avoid the torture?"

"We can't say that. Yet," she added after seeing Banks's expression. "I'd like to hear it from McCray. Which is why I'm here. His current location is classified. Can you clear it for me?"

Banks stared at her a long while before finally nodding. She could see in his eyes that he'd made some kind of decision, probably for his own benefit.

"Only so we can nail O'Reilly." He picked up the file. "I've been looking through his record. Although they've been considered successes on paper, each mission was beset with problems. Unexpected incursions. Bad data. If it wasn't for the luck of the Irish, I'd bet O'Reilly would be dead a dozen times over, with many of our best operatives."

"Yes, we have been having trouble with missions," she acquiesced. "It could be that the enemy is getting better and quicker than we are—"

"Or they could have had inside information," Banks interrupted. "We can't say categorically who he is or what he's done. He could be—and to me it's looking more likely—not one of us."

"I can't argue with that."

"So, how long was O'Reilly with us?"

"Four years. With full access to everything."

"Wipe the bastard off the face of the planet."

"We should bring him in and ascertain his alignment. We can't start wiping out our field agents without proper evidence … people will think we have something to hide."

"We've all got something to hide. I hope you don't need to be reminded whose side you're on."

Henderson didn't respond.

"Keep me on the wire about any info that comes up," Banks continued. "And sort out this Williams confusion and get her cleared."

"Fine." Henderson stood and walked down the twisting

corridor to the logistics room, her mind full of concerns. She was betting her career on vague clues, only apparent because they didn't add up. There were personal agendas at play under the guise of loyalty. It had always been her job to challenge those, but now she was sinking into the mire with them and could drown unless she did something about it.

*

Banks picked up the phone and dialed. His face reddened as it switched through to voice mail. "Yeah, me again. They're looking for you. This lack of contact is …" He paused as a pair of agents walked by his office, stopping momentarily before splitting and heading off in different directions. Where they listening?

"I am feeling a squeeze. It is vital that when you get this message you call me directly and immediately. I suggest you keep a low profile." He slammed down the phone.

*

"Everything okay?" Palmer asked.

Henderson's face radiated an intense anger. "Follow me."

She turned to Price and called out to him. "You seem good at this stuff. Tell me when Banks's clearance has come through on McCray's classified location. We'll be in the crunch room."

"Will you both fit?"

Henderson led Palmer to a small, unmanned meeting room. A terminal sat on the central table surrounded by cheap plastic chairs. Henderson powered up the unit and logged in. She indicated for Palmer to sit at the keyboard. Palmer looked up at her uncertainly.

"Something's up," Henderson explained. "The more we dig, the less things make sense. Pull up the historical information we have on McCray."

Palmer's fingers danced over the keys. The data flowed out over the screen, page after page scrolling by.

Henderson folded her arms and stared at the information. "Jesus. Read it and get back to me with a summary." She then left Palmer alone to get to work.

Palmer started to highlight data and copy it into a spreadsheet. The information, although dense and voluminous, fell into order. The results of McCray's evaluation once back on home territory, although his health and fitness were excellent, showed deep psychological issues, with severe lapses of paranoia and delusion.

She then correlated the data with the medical database. Appraisal readings were all over the place with bizarre and disturbing vocal responses. The medication was extreme; he should hardly be allowed onto the streets. But yet he was. Why?

Palmer spun her pen around her thumb as she mentally sorted the information. Who else knew him? Other team members.

She pulled up the team list: O'Reilly, Camden, McCray, and another four names. The first of the other four was normal, and still out in the field. As was the second. The third had showed signs of PTSD, and was now retired on a military health pension. Fourth had the records archived. Chris Adams. She checked the Date of Death, but nothing showed up. That was unusual. Why was he archived?

She picked up the phone and dialed.

"*Archives.*"

"I'm looking for the address of agent Chris Adams."

"*Certainly.*" Keys tapped in the background and then stopped. "*What was your name again?*"

"Palmer. Verity Palmer."

"*I'll have to take a note of that. We cannot assist you.*" The line disconnected.

Palmer stared at the receiver in disbelief. She pulled up the data on the other team members. They all had addresses and contact points.

"How's it going?" Henderson said as she leaned into the office.

"The strangest thing happened," Palmer reported. "I was checking on an address for a team member, which had been archived, and the guy in Archives went weird and hung up on me."

"Archives? I know them. Call them back."

Palmer picked up the handset and pressed the redial button. Henderson pressed the loudspeaker button. "I'll do the talking. What's the name?"

"Adams."

"*Archives.*"

"Is that him?" Henderson whispered. Palmer nodded. "It's Sandra Henderson, NCS Counterterrorism Intelligence, Lead. Who is this?"

"*Richard Lim.*"

"Ah, Richard, you remember me? I was Head of IA a couple of years back."

"*Uh, yeah.*"

"My associate Verity Palmer called you regarding some information regarding agent Adams. I'm after his current address. Read it out to me, would you."

"*I can't give you that information.*"

"Jesus, Richard, give me the address, or I'll come down there and rip it off your skin."

"*It's been redacted.*"

"Unredact it. I'm a level three and giving you authority."

"*It's from higher up.*"

"How much higher?"

"*Goodbye.*" The line disconnected.

"What is going on?" Henderson asked as the two women stared at each other.

"Have you come across Archives behaving like that before?" Palmer asked.

"No. And I deal with them a lot. Did you get a gist on Tank … McCray?"

"Yes. He's a mess," Palmer replied. "Highly unstable. Heavy medication and hardly had a sane thought in his head. Enough to lock up. But, he's not. That's why I was tracking down some of the team members to get another perspective." She pointed at the data. "He's all over the place. There's no way he should be out. So why is his location classified, when no one else's on the team is?"

"One thing you learn in IA—if you find a thread, pull it. Just out of interest, what happens when you run the addresses of the other team members through the news sites?"

Palmer entered the addresses into the database. "Nothing on ours. I'll check with police."

"Wait. What's that one?" Henderson pointed at a particular entry.

"Incident … gang firefight. Four months ago. Three fatalities on the exact street of one of the team lived on."

"Pull up the case file. Any pictures?"

A photograph of the victims flashed up onto the screen. They glanced between the victim file and the team member pictures. All victims' faces had been rendered into bloodied messes of cuts, bruises, and ruptures.

"It's too hard to tell," Palmer said.

"Pull in close on the figure on the left. The chest wound." Three bullet holes were centered over the heart in a tight group. "That is not a gangland 'firefight' hit."

Price ducked his head into the small room. "Clearance is through."

"Hallelujah. Give it to me," Henderson ordered.

Price smiled. Then stopped. "Dead."

"Dead end?"

"No. McCray's dead. You'd better come and see."

Henderson turned to Palmer. "Run the other addresses. Better yet, try and get in contact with the other members. See what comes up."

Henderson led Price back toward the logistics room.

"Adam McCray, AKA Tank, turned up on the Saudi Arabian east coast in March, near Dammam," Price said.

"Where was he before?"

"No record."

"Really?"

"This is exactly the kind of anomaly IA should pick up," Price suggested.

Henderson gave him a withering glare as they entered the room. "Thanks for that."

"Oh, yes. I forgot. We're at a dead end."

Henderson tapped her fingers on a desk. "Maybe not. Keep trying to crack what happened to McCray. I've got another lead."

10

SEAN PARKED THE scooter outside the TOT offices, which were already filling up with workers.

He and Lindsey swiped their passes on the card reader and pushed through the front doors. Sean spotted the security center positioned to the right of the foyer. The central stand was unattended, with people swiping themselves through. Past security, he spotted the services room.

"The key is to look confident," he whispered to Lindsey.

Sean strolled into the services room. Lindsey mimicked his style. Lockers lined one wall, with a bench on the opposite. He forced open the nearest locker and found a uniform that suited Lindsey. It took him an extra three to find one that came close to matching his size.

Wearing the uniforms over their own clothes, they grabbed cleaning equipment and peered into the foyer.

"Will anyone recognize you?" Sean asked.

"Will anyone recognize the dull brunette from Accounting who spoke to no one?"

"Lead the way."

"To where?" she asked.

"Anywhere where we can get into the system."

Lindsey headed into a large open plan office space housing a hundred cubicles that dominated the eastern wing of the building. She and Sean skirted around the edge of the cubicles, looking for anyone getting up to leave. Lindsey nudged Sean and pointed to an elderly lady rising to her feet next to a small meeting room. She held in her hands a heavily stained coffee mug covered hand-painted flowers.

They waited as the lady distanced herself from her desk. Keeping behind her field of vision, they approached the cubicle. Lindsey sat on the ergonomic chair in the old lady's workstation. The company insignia floated around the computer screen.

"Do they use complex passwords?" Sean asked.

"Yes. Letters and numbers, changed every two months. It was a pain."

"Statistically, most people use the name of family members." Sean glanced at the pictures sitting by the side of the terminal. They contained multiple generations of family members. It wasn't going to be a favorite niece. "We'll never guess it."

He then searched through draws for obscure words with numbers written on a piece of paper, but couldn't find anything. Lindsey hit the spacebar on the terminal. A login box displaying the company crest popped up in the center of the screen.

"Any ideas?" she asked.

He pointed toward the exit. The old woman was coming back. Sean scrawled the handset number on a Post-it note. "I've got an idea."

Lindsey pushed away from the desk, and Sean led her into the small meeting room behind the cubicle.

"Let me know when she sits and unlocks the computer," he said.

Lindsey wiped down the glass door and watched the old lady ease down and fiddle with her arrangement of pictures. Eventually, she unlocked the computer and started to type. "Okay, she's in."

Sean pulled out his phone and dialed, switching into a flat local accent as the call was answered. "This is reception," he said. "Your access card has come up with an error on your last swipe. Please present yourself immediately to the head of security."

Lindsey watched out of the corner of her eye as the old lady rose and hurriedly walked toward the reception. "Okay. She's gone."

She darted over to the desk, with Sean following, and reached for the mouse. Then she opened the browser and brought up the company intranet. "They've changed the system. It must be the dreaded upgrade they were always threatening us with." Even still, with a couple of clicks, Lindsey had opened the office database.

She studied the screen. "Okay, give me the number." Sean passed over the phone displaying the phone number he'd gotten from Hans, and she entered it. "Success."

"Can you trace it?"

"No, this woman doesn't have sufficient access. But I got the registered address. It belongs to this guy." She scribbled the name and address on a Post-it note and handed it to him.

Sean examined the piece of paper. "I know him."

"What's going on here?" said a voice behind them. Sean spun around to see the woman standing there with her hands on her hips.

"Sorry. She was feeling faint," he said, pointing at Lindsey.

Lindsey stood, turning bright red, and they moved toward the exit. Sean watched the woman over his shoulder.

The elderly lady sat at her desk and adjusted the items on her desk. She hesitated, staring at her Post-it notepad. Grabbing a pencil, she brushed the side of the lead over the pad and revealed the name and address. She glanced up, and her eyes met with Sean's. She reached for the phone.

"Move it," Sean said and he and Lindsey strode out of the office.

"Security, please detain the two cleaners leaving right now. I will be there immediately," the elderly lady said into the phone as she ripped off the top leaf of the pad.

She got up and hurried after them. As she approached the security checkpoint, the guard smiled at her. "Where are they?" she asked.

"The cleaners? They didn't come this way."

She glanced at the yellow square of paper. "Can I have your phone, please?"

The guard handed the telephone to her, and she dialed.

"Hello, police? I have suspicious activity to report," she said. "And an address for you to investigate."

*

Ireland
Location: Isolated Farm
Year: 1995
Time: 0315

Joseph and three heavyset prisoners bundled Sean into the back of a small van. It was a squeeze. The van bounced along the deserted streets and disappeared out of the city into the countryside. After passing a tiny house with a single light in the window, they turned off the road into a field containing a shed.

The wind howled through the tin sheets forming the shed's walls, cutting into Sean's bones. He'd only been allowed his prison uniform, although the others were dressed in thick clothing and enjoyed watching his discomfort.

A man walked out the shadows, himself a slender outline, his features hidden until he neared Sean and stepped into the light. The slight man wore a zipped-up navy jacket and dark brown pants, and had a set of oversized glasses perched on the bridge of his nose. He had close-cropped curly brown hair and a neat beard. The man appeared no more dangerous than an accountant. It was the same man from the prison, the governor's friend.

I've seen you before, Sean thought.

And the man who had stood next to the governor smiled and nodded. "Big Joe," he said. His voice seemed loud in the cavernous space.

"Sean, I'd like you to meet—" Joseph began.

"Liam," Sean finished, snarling the name. The recollection of the excessive pints and the brawl that ended with him in prison surfaced at the forefront of his mind.

"You know him? He is the Chief o' Staff."

"Chief of what?"

"The Irish Republican Army," Joseph added.

"You must be fucking kidding me." Sean swiveled on his heels and stared up toward the ceiling.

"Hello, young man," Liam said. He held out his hand. At first, Sean didn't move. "We meet again."

Joseph bumped his elbow into Sean's back. "Don't be rude."

Sean shook hands with the Liam without making eye contact. Liam's shake was firm, and his hand was calloused.

"How long have you been in jail?" Liam asked.

"Two years. Out of seven," Sean replied.

Liam shook his head. "It's a long time. The wrong place to whittle away your youth. You should be out drinking and cavorting with the ladies."

"Yeah, well, that didn't end up too good last time I tried. I seem to recall it being your fault."

"I don't remember holding a gun to your head and telling you to beat that young boy to death. You managed to do that all yourself. But I feel bad for you. I know some people. Maybe I can help you."

Sean paused. For two years, his life had been a constipated, bleak existence, where day-to-day survival had to be squeezed out. The best he'd got was better skills to manage the bleakness. No one had offered hope.

"You're a good Irish boy, ain't you? Proud of your country," Liam continued. "Good to your ma. That kind of thing."

"Yeah. What of it?"

"Let me explain some things to you. We live in a time where the enemy ain't so easy to detect. But that goes both ways. We fight small skirmishes here and there, but it's all small-minded and reactionary. We need a long-term strategy, one where we make a visible difference."

"What, like amnesty?"

Liam smiled. "We need people on the inside. We'd like to offer you a chance to blow the stinking Brits back to Holyhead, maybe even take the fight to them on their own hallowed green and pleasant fucking land."

"Jesus, you want me to be a spy?" Sean asked.

"Not a spy. We leave that title up to the hotshots at MI6 and their new best friends at the CIA. No, we need crusaders."

"But the fucking IRA? I want to have a clean life after I get out."

"After? Jesus, Joe, didn't you tell him? You'll be lucky to make it out, Sean. You can only fight the Proddies with your bare hands for so long until someone bigger, faster, and harder comes along. And there always is one. If you stay there, then you will die. And it won't be pretty." Liam pulled his collar up against the wind. "And say by some miracle you do survive the seven years and get released, you need to understand the reality of returning to the wider population. You've got a record. What kind of job are you going to get?"

The shed fell into a silence only punctuated by the wind. Liam let Sean brood on the ramifications.

"However, I can get you out. Tomorrow. With a clean record. You come work for us."

"I'm not interested," Sean insisted.

Joseph coughed. "Think about it, lad."

"You need to be interested," Liam said. "And engaged. We live in a time where you and your family members are easily found. And if the wrong person found your brother or your mother …"

Sean shot his fist at the small man, stopping shy of his jaw. "Don't you threaten my family."

"I am outlining the possibilities that you are going to be faced with if you choose poorly," Liam replied as he placed his hand around Sean's fist and lowered it.

"I'm not going to be a fucking spy."

"You enlist, and reap the rewards with the protection of your family, plus some good pay, or … well, you don't want anything to happen to your family, do you? I can't say it any clearer than that."

Sean glared at Liam. But what could he do? He spat on the ground at Liam's feet then nodded.

"Good lad," Joseph said.

"And get my brother out as well," Sean demanded.

Liam smiled. Joseph placed his hand on Sean's shoulder to lead him away. They paused as Liam continued.

"The Brits need to believe, and I cannot emphasize how important this is, they *must* believe you are one of them. And they will be listening to everything you do. I recommend you never speak with your family again. Because when they aren't listening, we will be."

*

United Kingdom
Location: London / Vauxhall Bridge
Year: 2000
Time: 1030

Joseph handed over a plain brown envelope. Sean glanced inside: passport, cash, driver's license. The wind whipped up the Thames as the two men huddled on the Vauxhall Bridge. A double-decker tourist bus, mostly devoid of any passengers, rolled past.

"We have a contact in Peckham," Joseph explained. "She's got a room for you while you settle in. She's okay with the Irish, just don't tell her you're black." He gave Sean a smile.

Sean laughed. "Despite obvious appearances of being as white as the snow."

"She's English. Prejudice blinds people to the truth."

Sean paused, taking in the hustle of the tourists. "Thanks for everything. I wouldn't have made it without you."

"We look after each other. Now with all these factions, we need something to galvanize the people. We're worse than a Proddy family with all the infighting. We'll never be free if we continue to argue among ourselves. We've spoken about this.

Liam has his objectives. It's important to remember the bigger picture."

Sean nodded. His life was getting complicated and was going to increase by another factor as soon as he entered the building.

"River City," Joseph said, pointing at the iconic building. "The Secret Intelligence Service is waiting for you, Michael Flanagan. Let your charm do its thing."

Rain fell from the gray skies. Joseph opened his black golf umbrella. He didn't offer any shelter to Sean.

"Won't they be suspicious?" Sean asked.

"They're not as intelligent as their moniker states," Joseph replied. "Many people have sacrificed a lot for this. You are our best bet for ending the dispute."

"By ending, do you mean winning?"

"It's a fight we refuse to lose. Look what the cost has been over the decades. What happened to 'Home Rule'? We're going to bring the bastards down. All you need to do is let us know what they know."

"You take care of me ma."

"Don't you worry. We'll keep an eye on her."

Joseph turned and left Sean staring up at the monolithic square building.

*

Thailand
Location: Bangkok
Time: 1045

Lindsey tapped Sean's shoulder and pointed at an old colonial house. The trees lining the promenade flicked shadows over the road as the scooter bumped down the uneven surface, past a van out the front of the house. They pulled around the corner and over the cracked pavement. The street remained quiet as morning sunlight filtered onto the tarmac. They dismounted and peered around the van toward the house. Lindsey leaned in close to Sean, peering over his shoulder.

"Who is this guy?" she asked.

"He's a dangerous man. I deal with him daily. He's the Captain's personal trainer," Sean replied.

"Who's the Captain?"

"My boss."

"And he sent his own man to kill you?"

"It looks that way. Let's find out."

Sean reached behind his back and pulled out his Beretta. He scanned the windows facing out into the street. They were all open, curtains drawn back or blinds raised. They waited until a car drove past, and then ran across the road. The front yard offered no coverage, causing them to charge up the steps onto the veranda.

The floorboards creaked. Sean sighed. The advantage was blown. He kicked open the door and dashed into the house. Rodriguez stood waiting in the corridor. He punched directly into Sean's path and missed. The two grappled, smashing against the walls. Pictures clattered on the hardwood flooring. Rodriguez capitalized on his position, swinging Sean around and tangling him up in one swift movement. Sean tumbled and crashed into a chair, which shattered under their combined weight.

Rodriguez clutched Sean's throat and squeezed. The men were locked together, struggling as their faces turning red. Sean's muscles started to fade. Rodriguez pushed his advantage and drove his fingers deep into Sean's throat. Sean flailed his hands against Rodriguez's face, searching for a purchase point, but his strength failed.

Then Rodriguez's eyes crossed, and he slid sideways revealing Lindsey behind him, with the remains of a smashed vase in her hands.

"I think I'm getting the hang of this."

*

Rodriguez tugged at his bonds as soon as he gained consciousness. He squirmed in the chair, twisting against the rope tying him down. Sean sat in a loose chair, watching him until exhaustion managed to achieve what Rodriguez's brain refused to accept. Lindsey stood behind Sean, keeping an eye on the front door. Rodriguez finally succumbed to his predicament and glared back at his captors. "What do you want?" he spat.

"Why'd you try to kill me?" Sean asked.

"You don't know what's going on? Man, everything is going to hell with this new Hydra deal. I got all sorts of shady people coming around my place uninvited. Although she's invited." He gave Lindsey a sleazy smile. Lindsey glanced over, giving him a look of distaste.

"I don't care about that. Why did you send the killers after me?" Sean pressed.

"What?"

"The contractors. Over in the *faran*. In the office?"

Rodriguez gave him a blank stare.

Sean sighed. "I was chasing Amanda's killer—"

"Who?"

Sean's voice tinged with frustration. "Jesus, *Amanda*. Brad's girlfriend."

"Who are these people?"

"I spoke about them with the Captain yesterday. You were there."

"I wasn't listening. You guys only talk shit." He attempted again to struggle free of the bonds. Sean waited until he calmed down.

"Listen, I got the phone of one of the contractors. It had

144

a number on it, which we tracked to your phone, to you."

"My phone?" Rodriguez said.

"Yeah, why did you send them after me?"

He laughed. "I didn't. My phone was stolen yesterday."

"You expect me to believe that?" Sean said.

"Why the fuck would I lie?"

"You're an evil bastard who'd do anything to get out of trouble. You expect me to believe someone is using your phone to send people to kill me?"

"You appear to have many friends. You don't believe me, then fucking call it. You won't hear it ringing around here. I got a new one."

"Where?"

"In my fucking pocket, you moron."

Sean frisked Rodriguez and collected a small feature phone from his back pocket. He checked the settings and confirmed it was a different number. He pointed the phone at Rodriguez. "Let me get this straight. Amanda is killed by someone who steals your phone. Isn't it all a little convenient? I follow them and then they turn up and try to kill me. It's someone you know."

Rodriguez rolled his eyes. "Ever since this Hydra deal turned up, everyone's been going crazy. Word has it that Ravens are getting it. The Captain is furious. He's doing everything to crush them, and losing his mind over it. You thought he hated them before. You should have seen him last night at training."

"What is it with this deal?"

"Big American players with bottomless pockets. It's going to change everything."

Wailing sirens filtered in from the road. Everyone's heads snapped around toward the door.

"You called the heat," Rodriguez shouted.

"Why would I call them?" Sean countered. "We are not the

kind of people who want their attention."

"Did he just call them 'the heat'?" Lindsey asked.

"Yeah," Sean replied.

"Does he think he's a gangster?"

"He is."

"Maybe I should've said gang*star*."

Sean turned back to Rodriguez. "How did they find us?"

Shouts came from around the house, front and back.

Sean stood and reached out for Lindsey.

"Hey, don't leave me here like this," Rodriguez shouted. He continued squirming, wrestling against the ropes.

The police burst in through the door. Sean grabbed Lindsey, and they tumbled to the ground and away toward the kitchen as more officers piled in through the rear entrance. They charged through the small bedroom and out into the corridor. Sean fired the Beretta into the air. The police dived for cover. Another policeman crashed into Sean and Lindsey from behind.

Several more shots rang out. Sean swung the smaller man off and landed a heavy blow on his jaw. The officer slumped over and Sean kicked him away. Rising, Sean noticed the bullet wound in Rodriguez's forehead, his eyes staring ahead.

Two police cornered Sean, brandishing Tasers. He kicked out, his foot catching one officer on his knee. The second lunged. Sean knocked aside the policeman's arm, pinning it against the wall with his forearm, and rammed his elbow into the chest of the first policeman. He twisted the Taser out of the first policeman's hand and discharged it into the second. The first crumpled as Sean planted one final kick into his groin. He then grabbed Lindsey and charged toward the front window, fired several shots through the glass, and dived through. They sprinted down the street and around the corner to the scooter.

Three police ran after them, shouting as their feet pounded the pavement. Sean told Lindsey to start the scooter as he turned and charged at the small group. The officers hesitated at his rapid about-face. He struck the first officer on the top of his skull, driving him to the ground. It was imperative that they didn't get past him to Lindsey, or their escape would be ruined.

The remaining two split, the first tackling Sean, the second dodging past him. He ignored the blows of the first and lunged after the second, bringing him down on the pavement. A sharp knee to the jaw of the officer hanging around his waist, and a vicious sledgehammer punch to the second policeman had them both down and out of operation.

Lindsey fired up the scooter and started to pull away. Sean ran up and jumped on behind, clutching onto her waist as she twisted the throttle to full. The three police officers groaned and squirmed, piled in the center of the road.

*

Back at Rodriguez's house, the police secured the area, roping the front door. Dumo and Jenna stepped over the barrier and glanced down the ruined corridor. They entered the front room, where Rodriguez sat dead, still tied to the chair. His head had fallen forward. Dumo examined the shattered window.

"He's gone," Jenna said. "O'Reilly."

"The man is as slippery as an eel."

Jenna examined the dead man. "Who was he?"

"Rodriguez Manus," Dumo replied. "Get headquarters to send through the intelligence on him."

"O'Reilly killed him."

"It certainly looks like it. Request forensics to do an autopsy to confirm."

A police officer approached Dumo with several items in evidence bags. Jenna examined the wall behind Rodriguez.

"Is this all you found?" Dumo asked, flicking through the bags.

"We are continuing the search, but this is all for the moment," the officer confirmed. "Plenty of drugs and cash. But there are no phones. None at all."

Dumo stared out the window in the direction Sean and Lindsey had run. "Mr. O'Reilly has a phone, one we can track?"

Jenna coughed. She'd extracted three bullets from the wall. She displayed them to Dumo in her gloved hand. "Without the autopsy, it's not certain what bullet killed him, but these bullets, which are probably in the same cluster, are not from a Beretta or any nine-millimeter pistol. They're ours, forty-five caliber rounds. And shot by a man who was unconscious." She indicated a nurse attending to the man still flat on the ground.

"Someone took the officer's gun?"

"Yes, judging by the trajectory. Then replaced it."

"You think it was O'Reilly?" Dumo asked.

"He had his own gun. Why use an unfamiliar one?" Jenna replied.

"The woman who is with him, what do we know about her?"

*

Henderson shook her head. If she were in a cartoon, she'd probably bang her head against the wall. And the wall would probably fall down. "All the addresses and contacts are cold?"

"Yes. All of them," Palmer reported. "I have a couple clues about Adams, but no one else."

Banks knocked on the door to the small meeting room. "A word please, Henderson."

She glanced up at him from her chair. "Clive, what are you still doing here?"

"What's going on?" he asked.

She paused. "You'll need to be more specific."

"Don't mess around with me."

"We're finding out about O'Reilly, and following up on

McCray for clarification."

Banks gave her another of his unsettling stares. She refused to flinch.

"*Archives.* Don't try to strong-arm other sections using your rank. If I get another call from Division, you'll find yourself without a pay grade." Banks then stormed off down the corridor.

Henderson and Palmer glanced at each other.

"I think we're getting close to something," Henderson said. "What do we do now?"

"We spoke to Archives about Adams. Like I said, when you find a thread, pull it. Grab your stuff, we're heading out."

"But you heard Banks," Palmer protested.

"And doesn't it concern you? Remember what's written above the entrance in big, golden letters carved into granite. THE TRUTH SHALL SET YOU FREE. We're going to follow the only lead we have and find Adams."

"The truth will also make you unemployed," Palmer said. "Or dead."

11

"**A**RE WE GOING to get in trouble over this?" Palmer asked. She held onto the panic handle as the GMC SUV skidded around the corner.

"Probably," Henderson replied. "What was the address again?"

Palmer repeated it for the fourth time.

"I have no idea where that is. I'm from Chicago. See if you can find it on the map." Henderson indicated a years-old street directory on the dash.

"Can't we use the GPS?"

"No, it's linked back to base. They'll be able to track us. Our advantage will be lost soon enough without us helping them."

Palmer glanced sideways at Henderson as she reached out for the large atlas and leafed through the index. "You'd better pull over so I can work out where we are."

Once they stopped, Palmer picked out the signposts and located the street in the directory. "Okay, I've got it. Let's go." Within ten minutes they were out in the suburbs and hurrying down the broad, leafy streets.

"This is Adams's address," Palmer said when they got close to their destination.

Henderson slammed on the brakes, and the GMC came to a shuddering halt. They stared at the plain Californian bungalow. It was quiet, the porch throwing the doorway into shade.

"Are you sure?" Henderson asked.

"From what I was able to work out from the data, this correlates as the location."

"So you're not sure."

"I'm sure enough. Let's go." Palmer opened the door and hurried across the road and up the garden path. Henderson curbed the GMC. Palmer approached the door but paused in front of it. As Henderson caught up, she also noticed the door wasn't locked but instead slightly ajar.

"Oh, my," Henderson said as they entered the house and made their way to the lounge. Shelves had been knocked over, their contents now strewn over the floor. All the seating cushions had been slashed open, then piled in the corner.

"I'm guessing Mr. Adams hasn't been home for a while," Henderson said.

"Burglary?" Palmer asked.

Henderson scanned the room. "Someone was certainly looking for something."

"Why do they have to be so destructive? I'm sure they could

achieve the same outcome by being methodical and neat."

"You search out back. I'll go through this room."

Palmer moved out to the kitchen at the rear of the building. Henderson could hear her opening the drawers and fridge.

"You find anything?" Henderson asked after a while.

"No," came the response.

Henderson joined Palmer in the kitchen. "Me neither."

"Adams has something important. People have searched for it. If I was a psychotic paranoid, where would I hide something?"

Mail sat piled on the kitchen bench. Palmer caught sight of the corner of a card emblazoned with the post office's insignia. She pushed aside the letters and picked it up. "I wouldn't keep it here." She checked the date on the card. Six months old. It tied in with the records of Adams' return. *Why would you leave something at the post office for months?*

"Where then?" Henderson said.

"The only place you can keep something safe under the full protection of the federal government."

"The post office."

Palmer nodded. "We're looking for a PO key."

They pulled open the cabinet doors and searched through the drawers. Henderson tugged out a collection of keys tied together. "Best bet," she said. "Where is the post card from?"

Palmer read the card. "It's the local branch."

They raced back out to the GMC and fired up the engine.

"Keep an eye out. Check that no one is behind us."

Palmer tilted her side mirror and watched back down the street. The road remained quiet. Not a soul moved. She wondered if it was too quiet.

Within ten minutes they were flicking through the keys for the one that fit into the postbox. Eventually, a key slipped into the small lock. Henderson glanced at Palmer and smiled. She turned the key, and the door sprung open. Inside was an A3 envelope bent over.

Henderson pulled it out. It had been sealed and had an imprint of a post office stamp over the flap. She slid her finger into the opening and sliced open the envelope, pulling out the contents.

"Medical records." She handed the papers to Palmer, who glanced over them.

"I've seen these before. They were the same ones recorded for McCray. The verbal responses are the same."

"So they've used Adams's results for McCray. Why?"

"The obvious answer is to make McCray appear unstable," Palmer said.

"Obvious, but unhelpful. So, if Adams was the unstable one, where is he now?" Henderson's IA instincts kicked in. *I've got to think about this. We're being watched, I can feel it.* "We need to move fast. Do we know where else he may be?"

Palmer raised the folder. "If these are his records, then he's in an institution."

*

United Kingdom
Location: Secret Intelligence Service Headquarters
Year: 2005
Time: 1400

A young man with slicked-back hair knocked on the partition and leaned into the nondescript cubicle. "Michael, HSO wants to see you."

Sean picked up his notepad and made his way to the level above. The lift opened into an enormous room, still steeped in 1960s architecture—a stark contrast to the modern, open plan, and plain floor below. Thick carpet rolled out toward an antique desk placed against the double-story windows that looked across to the anonymous north bank. Westminster Cathedral stood obscured by fog. It was as distant as his last meeting with Joseph.

Geri Madison, Head Special Ops assistant, sat behind her desk. She looked up and gave Sean a smile as he approached.

"HSO called for me," he said.

"You know what you have to say," Geri prompted.

Sean rolled his eyes as Geri closed hers. "How many loved your moments of glad grace, and loved your beauty with love false or true, but one man loved the pilgrim soul in you—"

"That'll do." Geri held up her hand and swallowed before breathing in deeply. "That *will* do."

"May I see him now?"

She sighed and pressed the door release. Resting on her elbow, she watched him walk into the office of the Head of Special Operations. "I'm free tonight if you want me."

Sean entered the room. It mirrored Geri's reception room in size and grandeur. The midday sun fell in through the towering windows and fell across the rich brown carpet. Portraits of previous commanders covered the far wall. A drinks table sat in the corner, tucked away from the light. HSO stood at the far side of his desk, reading a dog-eared file in an old plain brown folder. A red ribbon dangled over the folder's edge.

"You wanted to see me?" Sean asked.

"Have a seat." He called out for Geri to close the heavy oak doors. He waited until he heard the handle click into place.

"Times change. Our enemies, often less substantial than smoke, drift away. Generations change. Priorities change. The war moves on. And as ever, *Sember occultus.*"

"Am I being made redundant? Retirement?"

HSO smiled as he reached for a bottle of Chivas Regal. "I

don't think that will be possible. Drink?"

Sean shook his head. HSO poured himself a stiff couple of fingers into a crystal tumbler. The ice rattled around as he sipped.

"This morning we officially downgraded the IRA. In our consideration, they are no longer a major threat. They have new objectives, and now we have new directives from Number Ten and, as such, will be refocusing. And, as such, you can stop being Michael Flanagan. It always was a terrible name. Welcome back, Sean."

Sean raised his eyebrows and relaxed into the chair.

"You've been reading the internal memos about the Middle East?" HSO continued.

Sean nodded.

"We're concerned with some of the initiatives the CIA are implementing. Not only are they stepping wide of international law, but they're acting in ways our allies should not. It's always been our place to guide where we can, to let them know, as a good relative always should, when they are shoving their heads up their own arses. But they're not listening and have become worryingly isolationist."

"If, for some undisclosed personal reason, I wish to decline the opportunity, which you will eventually come around to?" Sean guessed.

"That would leave Intelligence in an awkward position. If people we'd been"—HSO waved his hand from side to side—"informing suddenly found out who we were and what we'd done, then the delicate network set up across Europe and the Middle East would be in jeopardy. And we couldn't have that. We'd have to offer up some symbolic gesture that you were suddenly found out to be a double agent."

"And I'd have to run?"

"The choice, of course, would always be yours. But your

potential sanctuaries are limited. Surely you don't want to live in fear on your own?"

Sean paused and peered out the expansive windows looking out across the Thames. "What about me ma?"

"You will have enemies. The IRA will be upset, but they're not what they were a decade ago. I'll guarantee they'll never know your circumstances for sure. We'll develop some credible story. She'll be all right if you keep your distance. But the danger hasn't changed, only the source."

"I'll need a new passport."

"Sorry, chum, can't help you with that. Maybe you could apply elsewhere. Maybe someone who specializes in supplying a new passport to people looking for a fresh start in life? Someone overseas?"

"How long have I got?"

HSO drained his glass. "How long do you need?"

*

"This is a nice place," Palmer said. The GMC idled as they examined the old two-story beachfront mansion fortified behind security fencing. "For a hospital."

The crisp white building had unparalleled views of the Pacific Ocean. Security patrolled around the building. Henderson killed the engine, and she and Palmer got out and watched the movement. Medical staff streamed out into the car park and several cars pulled into bays across the front of the house as they made their way toward the building. Henderson and Palmer showed their badges to the security as they approached the entrance, and were waved through. Inside, the staff were scanning their badges beside reception to enter the main area. Henderson and Palmer looked at each other. Their badges weren't going to cut it. They turned around and returned to the car.

"How do we get in?"

Henderson pointed at two doctors locked in a heated conversation in the car park. Their bags were placed between two cars, unwatched. "I'll distract them, and you get the bags."

"Are you going to undo your top?" Palmer asked with a smirk.

"This isn't the eighties." Henderson pulled her hair out of its ponytail and shook it free. "But men never change."

They strolled purposefully across the car park. Palmer broke away and circled the collection of cars. Henderson approached the men.

"Gentlemen," she started as she pulled a cigarette out of her bag. "Any of you got a light?"

She watched Palmer scoop up the bags and slip away. The men gave her combined expressions of disgust and intrigue.

"This is a medical facility. Smoking is banned here," the first doctor said.

"Nothing wrong with breaking the occasional rule. Isn't it good for your blood pressure?" Henderson asked.

"No, you're just polluting the air."

"We're outside. I can't pollute all the great outdoors."

Palmer reappeared and placed the bags down, with folded white material under her arm. She gave a thumbs-up.

"Excuse me, gentlemen," Henderson said as she squeezed between them. They watched her pass, then grabbed their bags and jumped into their cars.

"What'd you get?" Henderson asked when she regrouped with Palmer.

"Their passes and lab coats."

"Well done." They slipped on the coats and clipped the badges to their pockets. They then entered the facility and approached the reception. Desk nurses busied themselves with paperwork. More staff moved around the open area inside the security gate, pushing patients in wheelchairs, or assisting them walk.

"Jesus, how are we going to play this?" Palmer asked. "Can we flash our badges?"

"No. We can't raise any suspicions," Henderson replied.

"Is there anything else we can flash?"

Henderson smiled. "Just be cool. Follow me."

She sauntered up to the security gate and swiped her card. The gate unlocked, and she pushed her way through. Palmer followed. The gate clanged closed behind them. Palmer jumped.

Henderson called over an orderly. "I'm looking for Chris Adams."

The orderly pointed her in the direction of a group of youngish men sitting together who were staring out at the sea. Palmer scanned their faces for one that would be a match for the strong young man in the team photographs. All she saw was a bunch of timid shells, afraid to look at her face. She found the closest match, although his body was diminished and he hid his face behind long, unkempt hair.

Henderson sat down next to him. "Are you Chris Adams?"

The man looked away, swinging his head as if he'd heard a distant sound.

Palmer sat down next to Henderson. His head swung back and watched her out of his periphery vision. "Are you Chris?" she asked.

The man started to fidget, his fingers crushing and releasing the edge of his ward clothing. "Maybe," he replied.

"Chris, we need your help," Henderson said.

"A-a-are you a-a-agency?"

"Do you distrust the agency?"

"You're speaking funny, like them doctors." The man rocked slowly and incessantly in his chair.

"Yes." She looked over her shoulder at Palmer. "We are."

"She's a-a-a pretty one."

Henderson glanced over at Palmer. She was a natural stunner. Voluminous dark hair fell in curls around her angelic face. Bright, intelligent eyes. A body fit and trim from the agency's basic training. Henderson leaned over to Palmer and whispered, "Put your glasses on, you'll look more doctor-y. Try and be nice."

Palmer sat up straight and pulled her oversized reading glasses out of a shirt pocket. She leaned forward and Adams erupted into a fit of embarrassed giggling.

Palmer looked to Henderson. "Do we ask about what happened out in Abbottabad?"

"Good lord, no. That's what caused his PTSD." Henderson glanced around the room. "See if he knew where McCray lived."

"Could we …" Adams struggled with his words. "Could we d-d-d … go on a d-d-date?"

"I tell you what, Chris, I'd like you to help me first," Palmer said. "Could you do that for me?"

"Yeah. I'd-d like to h-h-help you."

She smiled and adjusted her glasses. He sneaked a few peeks at her face and hazarded a smile. "You remember Tank?"

"Yeah."

"Do you know where he lived?"

"H-h-he lived in secret."

Palmer half smiled. "Do you remember anyone who was his friend who wasn't in the agency? A friend, like we could be."

Chris let out a nervous laugh and stared at his feet. His rocking became more urgent. "Yes. Jim. H-h-he was a fr-i-end from college. H-h-he lived with Jim."

"Do you remember his full name?" She placed her hand on his knee. His intensity wound up tight, and he let out a quiet yelp.

"Jim Fellows. D-d-down in Gayme. H-h-he was a secret."

"Why was he a secret?"

"D-d-don't ask, d-d-don't t-t-t-t ..."

"No need to go on. I know what you're saying."

Henderson watched the man. He appeared so lonely. The brief interaction with Palmer had visibly lifted him. "Verity, could you look up the address?" She turned back to Adams. "Does anyone visit you in here?"

"No. Never."

"That's sad. What about—"

"Except yesterday."

Henderson paused. "Who visited yesterday?"

"Some man, came d-d-down a-a-asking the same questions a-a-as you. But I d-d-didn't tell h-h-him anything."

"Was he agency?"

"I d-d-don't talk to a-a-agency. Not a-a-about Tank."

"There they are," boomed a voice from across the room. The loud noise made Adams coil away, whimpering.

Henderson glanced up. It was the doctors from the car park. Palmer jumped up. Chris, sensing her concern, also rose. Out of his wheelchair, he was no longer the invalid tormented by a horrific past, but a soldier once again.

"Go," he said as he pointed at the fire exit. He approached the doctors with his arms out, screaming at them. Henderson pulled Palmer out the exit as the alarm rang out. The last thing they saw was Chris falling under the weight of several heavyset orderlies. They wrestled him to the ground and proceeded to beat him.

*

"Where have you been?" Price asked as the two women rushed in.

"Out at Gayme," Henderson snapped. "We found McCray's

159

house and his lover, who had some very interesting information."

"What did she say?"

"I'll explain in the meeting room, follow."

*

"Are you Jim Fellows?" Henderson asked.

The skinny man nodded.

Henderson and Palmer showed their badges to him. His face went pale.

"You are aware that Andy McCray has been reported, um, deceased?"

Jim sighed. "It was always a chance, every time he went out the door. It was terrible waiting for him, never knowing when—if—he'd come walking back in."

"We understand that this is difficult for you, but could you fill in some details? His demise has uncovered several anomalies within the agency."

"Come in."

Inside the apartment, Jim offered the women a seat. The shiny black shelves were populated with pictures of the two men, with their arms around each other.

"When was the last time you heard from Andy?"

"Beginning of February. He said he was laying low, his nerves were shot. He was heading to somewhere where he could work some things out."

"Do you know where?"

"He kept a secret phone, just for the two of us. I was able to see that he'd gone to Cape Town before he turned it off."

"Was he all right?"

"He wasn't the best of men, with his desires."

"Could you clarify that?"

"With the drugs and … boys."

Henderson paused. "I was speaking about his mental condition."

"What do you mean?"

"Did he suffer from PTSD?"

*

Palmer and Price sat at the small desk with the terminal, while Henderson stood nearby. Price started to fiddle with the keyboard. "Tank's records were faked," Palmer explained. "He wasn't paranoid delusional, just shit-scared and apparently a real low life. Do we have a safe house in Cape Town, South Africa?"

"I'll check. Safe houses are quiet, though," Price replied. He started typing. "I've already found a problem. This is secured data. If we pull it, a warning will be sent, probably to Banks."

"Fine, I'll distract him." Henderson hit the loudspeaker button and dialed.

"Jane Madison, Head of LA."

"Jane, Sandra Henderson here. How's it going? You settling into the position? Made lots of enemies yet?"

Madison laughed. *"You never told me I'd instantly be dropped from every party list. I assume this isn't a social call?"*

"Look, could you do me a favor. I think Banks has some confused information. We've been tracking several accounts through Bangkok, and we've been finding some private ones with significant assets linking back to Clive. It may be nothing. Maybe have a friendly word with him. It'll get you on my party list."

"You can't say that," Palmer whispered.

She smiled at Palmer. "It could be true. I'm sure it'll all be a misunderstanding."

"Really?"

"It may be nothing. I just need some clarity on it."

"We can schedule it in next week."

"We're watching significant transfers bouncing around now. Is it possible to have a word with him now? If they stop, then we'll know if it's tied to him," Henderson pressed.

"I'll send down a junior to book an appointment. That'll spook him if he's up to anything."

"Thanks, Jane. Consider yourself invited." She disconnected the call. "Hit it, Daniel."

Price logged into the system and started searching. "We have half an hour at the most. This is our only window of opportunity."

"Do you want me to do anything?" Palmer asked Henderson.

"Riddle me this: if O'Reilly called al-Qaeda so they could capture them—which I find hard to believe—how did we end up with the OBL location?"

"Luck. Maybe it didn't go down how he plan—"

"Wait. They were captured. Pull up the pictures sent out by al-Qaeda."

"Daniel is on the terminal," Palmer reminded her.

Henderson disappeared out the door and returned with an old monitor and console. Price connected the leads and powered up the unit. Henderson and Palmer fidgeted and spoke in broken sentences over the discovered facts. Price gave them a thumbs-up as the welcome screen appeared on the display. Palmer logged in and pulled up the photographs on screen.

"Now bring up his pre-mission photographs." Palmer placed the two pictures side by side. Henderson pointed at the screen. "Look at his face, before on the pre-mission briefing and after, when they posted his picture online. He has a scar under his eye."

"Like a tear," Price said, glancing over.

"Burned skin," Henderson confirmed. "Acid. He was tortured. The reports omit it. And I'd bet he didn't call them."

"So if he didn't call, who did?" Palmer asked.

Price sat up. "You need to check this out. I'm into the safe house database. Data is coming up on the screen."

A red security banner flashed across the Price's monitor.

"ADMIN HAS BEEN NOTIFIED." He sighed as he read out the warning. "It's on my login, too. Anyway, McCray entered

February 3, confirmed by CCTV images. The house is then accessed on February 10."

"By who?" Henderson asked.

"I don't know. There is nothing other than it opening with authorization. Like it was a ghost. No record of him checking out either. The door remained locked."

"A ghost with authorization. Get me a list of people who have the authority or ability to do that."

"McCray was in a safe house in Cape Town. Never checks out but ends up dead on the Saudi coast." Henderson went silent, tapping her fingers on the desk.

"What are you thinking?" Palmer asked.

"I'm thinking it was us. All of it." Henderson shook her head. "I can't believe we sold out our own men."

"It doesn't say that," Price said. "But as the situation arose where we could benefit, with the result being the address of OBL, then tactically it would have made sense. The numbers stacked up. It was worth the trade. Or risk, however you want to look at it."

"I can understand that, but what I'm having trouble with is that we sold out the cell to al-Qaeda. Tank found out and went to hide. Someone, one of us who is very senior, tracked him down and got rid of him."

12

INSPECTOR DUMO'S OFFICE was awash with paperwork, providing a challenge to answering the ringing phone. He waved the assistant out of his office and signaled for her to close the door.

A familiar distorted voice echoed down the line. *"O'Reilly doesn't appear to be pursuing Hydra."*

"He's still concerned about Amanda Sakda. As are we."

"*She is not important*," the voice replied. "*He needs to be guided. Send him a message.*"

"I'm not used to working in conjunction with other international organizations. Pardon my bluntness, but what's in it for us?"

A moment of silence passed before the voice continued, conveying frustration even through the distortion. "*If you proceed as planned, then you will be an international hero, having cracked one of the most powerful black-market dealers. Imagine, international praise being rained on your poor excuse of a department. Is that enough 'it' for you?*"

Dumo understood that lack of funds, poor pay, and difficult conditions didn't always provide the best of recruits, but they still performed the best they could under the circumstances. A point he was tired of arguing with his superiors, who didn't seem to suffer from the same deficiencies as the rest of the department. "You can confirm I will be allowed to arrest O'Reilly."

"*You will find the benefits of following him will outweigh the short-term achievement of his brief incarceration.*"

"Brief?"

"*There will always be someone who can bail out Mr. O'Reilly. Stop thinking so small.*"

"I'll get the techs to send a message. What needs to be said?"

The distorted voice switched to an automated voice as it read out a sentence. Dumo wrote down the message.

"And who is this from?"

"*Ichkeria-six.*"

"That's an odd name."

"*It will mean something to O'Reilly.*"

"Are you sure the contact would send this?"

"*He's under pressure. This will increase it. Yes.*"

13

RODRIGUEZ'S CELL PHONE buzzed. Sean parked the scooter and read the display. Lindsey took off her helmet and shook her hair free, letting the breeze cool down her head.

"What's it say?" she asked.

"It says, 'MEET MY CONTACT AT SUVARNABHUMI AIRPORT, UNDER CENTRAL CLOCK. SIXTEEN HUNDRED. ICHKERIA6'."

"Someone wants Rodriguez to meet a contact." Lindsey ran her fingers through the tangled ends of her hair. "What's that last word?"

"It's another name for Chechnya, with a six added on the end." Sean paused. "It says it's a trap."

"How could it be? Rodriguez is only just dead."

"I'm sure whoever is behind this has links into the police. Even listening on the police band will give them enough information to piece two and two together."

Sean stared at the name as the traffic streamed past. *Ichkeria-six.* It was Brad's codename for his first mission. HQ had sent him into Chechnya to blow up a rare earths refinery. He'd built his reputation on that mission. No one knew the codename. Certainly no one outside the agency. Sean only knew it because of the half-dozen missions he and Brad had run together. Sending this now was deliberate. It had to either be a hint, a message, or a trap.

"Not many people know this code." He glanced over at Lindsey. "It has to be a trap."

"What are you going to do?" Lindsey asked as she strapped back on her helmet.

"Fall into it." Sean slipped the phone back into his pocket and revved the scooter's little engine. "We go to Suvarnabhumi."

Banks burst into the crunch room, catching the team in deep discussion.

"What the hell are you doing?" he demanded.

Henderson, Palmer and Price all raised their heads in unison. Only Henderson feigned a believable expression of confusion, while the others radiated guilt. "We're trying to find Sean O'Reilly. As you asked."

"I just had IA poking around in my office asking questions that were inappropriate and highly suspicious."

"Nothing to do with me, or us. I'm sure it was just a misunderstanding. Although IA rarely asks inappropriate questions."

Banks glared at Henderson, who looked back, wide-eyed. The red security banner flashed across the Price's monitor.

"What's that?" Banks' attention had been broken. This was her chance to keep him off balance.

"We've been getting that a lot in the last half hour. Sean appears to have security issues all over the place. I know Jane, my replacement in IA. Do you want me to have a word with her?"

"Just get me answers."

Henderson and the others then watched Banks storm back toward his office.

"We're skating on the thinnest ice ever," Price said once their boss was out of earshot. "And it's about to get worse."

Henderson's face contorted in confusion. "Meaning?"

"You know how you said Beck Williams was on long service?"

"Yeah?"

Price pointed at a line of code in the file dump. "Why did she log into the system two days ago?"

"How on earth did you find that?"

"I don't know why she's done this, but she's used the same code on the fertilizer factory as she did on Abbottabad. I've been able to decode what she did."

"And?"

"Are we meant to be looking at this?" Price asked. "Because Banks seemed pretty adamant that we keep away from the fertilizer factory."

"Leave Banks to me. Just show me what you found," Henderson insisted.

"This goes way higher than Banks. Williams was watching the mission."

"Why?"

"Unfortunately, she didn't leave notes regarding her inner thoughts," Price said. "She typed a couple of lines which she then deleted. *Mission compromised. Six awoke. Neutralized. Proceed or decept?* Then, she cut out Robinson and replied: *Decept.*"

"What mission? Because it's obviously not the one Brad was on. 'Six awoke.' Six must have been Brad. He learned something."

"Beck Williams ordered the death of one of our men?" Palmer asked.

"What would someone learn out at a fertilizer factory that a senior head at the CIA would kill him over?" Henderson wondered.

"Also …" Price began.

"There's more?"

"The people listed on this message. Brad was Six, as you worked out. And Four was played by Frank Jensen. You remember the internal memo that circulated a few days ago when Jensen turned up dead?"

"So who was playing Four? It certainly wasn't Frank Jensen."

"I hate to point this out, but if Jensen was assassinated three days ago, I would be inclined to think that Williams had something to do with that as well."

"She couldn't be FOUR, could she?" Palmer asked.

"Williams is fifty-five and has been in management, schmoozing politicians at expensive dinners, for fifteen years. She couldn't be FOUR, but she'll damn well know who is," Henderson replied. "Jesus, Brad. What did you get yourself wrapped up in?"

*

Great sails stretched over the curved roof floating above the concourse at Savarnabhumi. Those waiting for arrivals stared up at the enormous monitors, oblivious to the maelstrom of humanity buzzing around. Sean snaked through the crowd, keeping an eye on the security patrols. Petty crime had increased in the terminal and patrols had multiplied to ease the concerns of paying tourists.

He spotted the central clock, a glass and steel cubic construction suspended from the roof, and visible from every point on the concourse. Sean slowly approached the centerpiece. Through the milling travelers, he was unable to see anyone stationary. He steered into an open bookstall with a rotating display of science-fiction paperbacks. He picked up a Stephen King book then realized its cumbersome thickness was suspicious. It was more a blunt weapon for bludgeoning than airplane reading. He picked up an old retro book, blissfully thin, and opened to the middle pages while keeping an eye on the clock.

Sixteen hundred hours came, and no one appeared and remained under the clock. One past. Two past. Still no one. A tour group swarmed down the escalators and along the concourse. As they dispersed among the shops, he spotted the back of a heavyset man in a brown leather jacket. He stood to one side of the clock and glanced at his wristwatch.

Sean rubbed his eyes. The brittle light streaming through the windows blurred his vision and disguised the details of the man. He moved closer.

The anonymous man continued to stare in the opposite direction. His stance was familiar. Sean dropped the book onto a seat and approached him, keeping passing traffic between them.

The man turned, leaving few places Sean could hide. He ducked and feigned tying his shoe. He had to process the face he'd just seen and what it meant. He'd seen one name and now could tie it to a face.

Keeping his head down, Sean pulled out Rodriguez's phone and dialed.

After several rings, the man reached into his pocket and pulled out his phone. He smiled as he saw the number on the screen.

"Rodriguez, where are you?" The man started to spin around, looking out through the crowd. "You're late"—He then came face-to-face with Sean, who also holding a phone to his ear—"again."

The man slipped his phone into a pocket at a slow, measured pace. "Who the fuck are you?"

"Hello, Chanchai," Sean said.

"How'd you know my—?"

"What are you doing here?" Sean stepped forward, bearing over the shorter man, who reeled back from the sudden aggression.

"Always on the lookout for a good deal," Chanchai replied. "I like to travel. You often hang out in airports, snowflake?"

"Checking out escape routes." Sean gave him a fleeting smile. He raised the phone. "This belongs to Rodriguez, who works for the Captain. I don't think I've seen your face around."

"You work for the Fleet? Jesus. For a second I was worried."
Chanchai stepped back, smiling and loosening his shoulders.

Sean tensed as he picked the subtle facial twitches of an overconfident man. A tightening jaw, hard swallow, right shoulder dip. The crowd lulled. Chanchai was about to pounce. Sean dodged backward as Chanchai slipped out a knife and stabbed at Sean's stomach. Sean intercepted and deflected the blow, swinging his own arm around and locking Chanchai's. He twisted the other man's wrist and forced open the hand. The knife clattered on the tile flooring, and Sean kicked it away under a row of seats.

Sean then caught sight of a black mark on the inside of Chanchai's wrist. Pulling back the man's sleeve revealed a black bird tattooed to the inside of his arm.

"You're a Raven."

"So what?"

Sean twisted Chanchai's wrist harder and forced him into the entrance of a service corridor out of direct view. "I've got to ask what a loyal employee of the Captain is doing meeting with a minion of his absolute enemy."

"Loyal?" Chanchai pulled himself free. "There is no loyalty anymore. We're looking out for ourselves."

Sean circled around Jaide's henchman, keeping a close eye on his hands. "You killed Amanda."

"Who?"

"The girl."

Chanchai shrugged. "Lot of girls in my life. Most of them end up dead when they get too needy."

"Last night. You and someone else over in the *faran* sector."

"Can't remember."

"Let me help you." Sean stepped in, using his superior height to intimidate the man. "Was it Rodriguez?"

"Fuck no. That pussy would never turn up to something

like that. It needs someone with more balls."

"Then why have you got his phone?"

"The dumb fucker leaves it all over the place. It's been fun watching him struggle with his lost contacts." An obvious fact sunk in. "You called me on his new phone. Why have you got it?"

"As you said, he leaves them all over the place," Sean replied.

"Where is he?" Chanchai glanced at his wristwatch.

"Am I keeping you from something?"

"You'd better give me that phone," Chanchai hissed.

"Come take it."

"With pleasure."

The men scuffled in the narrow corridor. Their arms slipped and intertwined, each man searching for a secure hold. Sean found a wrist lock and pulled his opponent close.

"Why'd you want his phone?" The grip slipped, but Sean thrust his hand around Chanchai's throat and pushed the smaller man against the wall.

Chanchai didn't respond. His face reddened as struggled to free his neck. Sean squeezed. And his prisoner caved.

"There's a message in it."

"So who's Ichkeria-six?"

Chanchai shrugged again. "It's hard to keep up with all the attention. You know how it is when you're popular. Oh, I forgot. You wouldn't know."

He'd made the joke too soon. Sean shook the man and drove his thumb deeper into the man's throat.

"I don't buy it. Who's Ichkeria-six?" Sean pressed.

"No one. Just some new hotshot making waves on the scene. I don't know who."

Sean sensed the change in Chanchai when he mentioned the name. Underneath the bravado, the man was uncertain, afraid. Chanchai glanced down the corridor toward the entrance.

People flashed by, unaware of the struggle. Concern etched into the smaller man's face.

"You seem mighty nervous," Sean noted. "Are you waiting for someone? Maybe Ichkeria-six?"

"It's no business of yours. Just piss off."

A security patrol wandered past, giving them a casual glance before he paused. Sean released Chanchai and stepped clear. The guards turned away, keeping an eye on them, and continued on.

"Wait. You're waiting for Rodriguez at the airport?" Sean asked.

Chanchai then sprinted out of the corridor back into the concourse. Sean charged after him and grabbed his jacket. He felt something bulky in the pocket. Sean pulled out the contents. He fanned out the items in his hand. People slowed to watch the confrontation.

"Passport. Business class ticket to Brazil. Why are you leaving? More importantly, why are you leaving with Rodriguez?"

"Give those back." Chanchai lunged forward, wrapping his hand around Sean's wrist. The two twisted through several locks until they ended up in a stymie.

"What's going on?" Sean demanded.

"You got no idea. Everything is about to change. It's going to get dangerous around here. Hydra is going to change everything. If you had any sense, you'd be getting out before it's too late."

Voices rose around them, calling for security, and people backed away.

"Who's Hydra?"

"Who the fuck knows," Chanchai replied. "Hydra is Hydra. Just another big American syndicate. Between them and the Russians, the black market is flooded."

"So is Ichkeria-six linked to Hydra?"

Chanchai grabbed the ticket and turned to run, but Sean snatched his collar and pulled him back. "I'm going to ask you one more time; who is Ichkeria-six?"

"I don't know. He's just a message on the phone. He pays cash. He pays up front."

"What's he been asking for?"

"Information about what Jaide is doing, about what the Captain is doing."

"Bullshit. Mysterious people don't pay fifty grand for some info on part-time drug dealers." Sean could hear whistles.

"They want nerve gas, that Kolokol shit. Not a huge amount, but enough for someone to break into the industry."

"What do they want it for?"

"We're getting cash, so we don't ask questions."

Someone bumped past Sean, and he heard the familiar sound of compressed gas. A silencer used at close range. He waited for the shock to hit him but his senses stayed neutral. He hadn't been shot. Chanchai slumped down, clutching his stomach. Blood seeped out through his fingers.

A woman screamed as she saw the blood spill over the floor. The security patrol turned around and spotted the incident. One reached for a two-way radio clipped to his belt while another pulled out a small pistol.

"Drop your weapon," the guard ordered.

"I don't have a weapon," Sean shouted. They ran toward him, struggling against the churn of the escalator.

14

S EAN SPRINTED TOWARD the glass sliding doors that formed the entrance to Suvarnabhumi. They were shutting, trapping him inside. Queuing travelers screamed and leaped for cover as he pulled out the Beretta and fired, shattering the glass. It rained onto the floor as he slipped through the opening. Lindsey stood by the scooter.

"Start it," he shouted.

"It died," she replied.

Sean fumbled with the controls, but the engine refused to spark. Shouts from the security guards caused them to abandon the vehicle and sprint into the car park. They outpaced the overweight guards, but two fit guards kept up with their blistering pace. Lindsey and Sean followed the curve of the driveway up to the next level and searched for another scooter. Gunfire sent them behind the parked cars for cover.

"Are security guards allowed to fire?" Lindsey shouted.

"Welcome to Bangkok. It could be worse. If we were drug runners, then they would be using machine guns."

"Any success?"

"Sort of."

The security guards ran past and up onto the next level. Sean and Lindsey watched the guards go by. They dashed down to the lower level, running directly into the slower guards as they rounded the corner.

Lindsey and Sean ran to the railing and jumped down to the basement level, then sprinted down the concrete ramp, leaning into the corner as it twisted down. Sean thought Lindsey would be struggling by now, but she was matching him stride for stride. It was unusual. The shouts behind them got louder. Engines roared, and sirens rang out. A car backed out of a parking bay, causing them to leap over the hood. Lindsey slipped as her laces tangled on the hood ornament. She fell, crashing onto the concrete. Sean turned and scooped her up, and the two ran off with Lindsey limping.

The stairs up to the arrival terminal lay ahead. If they could get inside, they could find cover. Lindsey leaned on Sean, placing her full weight on him and grimacing as the pain speared through her ankle.

Twenty meters and they would be out of immediate danger. Ten. Then police cars roared in from either side of the entrance and one in behind, blocking the exit. A handful of police ran down the stairs with their weapons drawn.

Sean and Lindsey raised their hands. Two officers ran up and wrenched off Sean's backpack and yanked his hands behind his back. Handcuffs snapped over his wrists. They repeated the action on Lindsey, who attempted to balance on her good ankle. The police vehicles backed up to clear a path. A sergeant opened the rear door of the closest patrol car. As Sean's head was pushed down into the back of the vehicle, gunfire exploded behind them.

The basement filled with squealing tires. More gunfire rang out, this time, closer. Bodies went down behind him, followed by screams of pain. A masked man hauled Sean out of the car by his jacket. A second man scooped up his backpack and threw it in the back of a nearby black van. Two more men in balaclavas shouted at Sean to get into the vehicle. One grabbed Lindsey and shoved her into the back. She struggled to stay upright and toppled onto the metal floor.

A bag dropped over Sean's head. Lindsey gasped as the same happened to her. The fusillade continued in staccato bursts. The pitch of the fire indicated at least three semi-automatics were being used. A heavy object thumped on the floor of the van. The doors slammed closed, and the van's tires shrieked as the vehicle spun around and headed out of the car park. The gunfire faded away.

"What's going to happen?" Lindsey asked.

"No talking!" one of the men ordered.

"Don't worry. They don't want to kill us," Sean said in a soft tone. "It'll be interesting finding out who they are."

"We're not still with the police?"

"No."

"I said, no talking!" the man repeated.

The van bumped along the road careening around corners. Eventually, the driving settled down. Someone tuned the radio to a local station.

The van soon came to a halt. Fresh air flooded into the cabin. Rough hands grabbed Sean and Lindsey once more and pulled them out of the vehicle. Lindsey stumbled as she landed on the ground. They were thrust forward, Sean running and Lindsey limping to avoid falling again.

The manic pace continued as they were led along corridors, into a lift, then out. Sean could sense the large area they'd been brought into. A man kicked the back of his legs and he was forced onto his knees. The cord around his neck tightened then released. The bag was pulled free, and the bright lights forced him to look down. He blinked until the sensitivity in his eyes eased. Lindsey, by his side, paled and her eyes widened.

They were in a hotel conference hall, populated with the occasional piece of furniture and several men holding them at gunpoint. They all removed their masks, revealing themselves to be locals. None of them looked familiar. A 1960s egg chair sat on the opposite side of the large glass desk. An eight-foot cutout of a black bird sat secured to the far wall with thick bolts.

"Jesus, it's you," Sean said.

A slender woman swiveled around in the egg chair. She wore a gold dress that offset her complexion, making her look radiant. Her dark hair fell into a widow's peak that framed her elegant features. Her legs were crossed, exposing her knees. She gracefully stood, the expensive material falling into place without her having to adjust it.

"I hear you've been looking for me," she said.

"Who is it?" Lindsey whispered.

"Jaide Gabat. Daughter of Harry Gabat. Leader of the

Ravens. I've been trying to kill her," Sean replied.

"Why?"

"The Captain wanted her dead."

"Any idea why?"

"I don't ask questions."

"Well, that skipped the need for formal introductions. You want to know why?" Jaide asked.

Sean shook his head. "Not really."

"Hydra. Someone is going to break into the weapons market with this new contract. And it's going to be us. The dear Captain believes that if he can kill me, then the contract will fall to him. Deluded fool. He really fails to think clearly, objectively about things. Always so emotional." Jaide then glared at Sean. "What were you doing meeting with Chanchai?"

"I'm trying to find the person who killed my friend's girlfriend. The trail is leading to you," Sean replied.

"Me? I didn't kill anyone. What was she to me?"

"Why did you kill Chanchai?"

"Again. It wasn't me."

"Then who killed him?"

"You may be surprised to know how little I care."

"Wasn't Chanchai always working for you?" Sean asked.

"Yes. For years."

"I'm not sure how long it's been going on, but he has been setting something up with one of the Captain's senior men."

Jaide let out a disappointed sigh. "I thought he was loyal."

"He'd been giving inside information on you to someone called Ichkeria-six."

"I've never heard of them."

"An agent of Hydra."

She changed, her face turning hard. "Now I wish I had shot him. Double-dealing scum."

"It turned out Chanchai had been feeding the Captain

information on you for years. But something changed in the last couple of days. A new high bidder."

"That sneaky little bastard. I see that times have become desperate, and my hand is forced." Jaide turned to the assembled henchmen. "It's time for the Ravens to diversify."

"I thought your father didn't want to do that," Sean said.

"That's where you come in. His ideas are old-fashioned, as is he. We need to move forward and we can't with him at the head. You are going to kill my father."

Sean laughed. "No."

One of the guards snapped forward and smacked a small cylinder against Lindsey's neck, making her cry out.

"Your girlfriend has just been poisoned with venom of the something or other, or something," Jaide explained. "You want to save her, then you need to kill Harry."

"Why me?"

"Why does a henchman of the Captain have to kill my father, rather than his daughter? Surely I don't need to answer that."

"Fine. Where is he?"

"The central hospital. Ward A-37. He's on life support so even you will be able to do the job. I'll send flowers." Jaide glanced at her wristwatch. "You've got about two hours before your girlfriend dies. I suggest you hurry. It's a thirty-minute walk from here. Tell Father we used the red cylinder. He'll be able to tell you which among his myriad of bottles is the correct antidote."

A henchman pulled Sean up and unlocked the handcuffs. He wrung some life back into his wrists. "He'll tell me when I'm about to kill him?"

"You'll work it out."

*

Harry Gabat wheezed through an oxygen mask. His eyes hung heavy. The private ward was palatial and secured, and it took several minutes to assess the flow of the staff and pinpoint a moment to enter unseen. Harry's eyes opened wide. He pulled down the mask to talk. "Who are you?"

"Sean O'Reilly. Your daughter sent me."

Harry let out a slow laugh, which sunk into a cough. He replaced the mask and controlled his breathing until his body stopped shuddering. His face paled as the color drained.

"Jaide's poisoned a friend of mine," Sean continued. "She said you'd be able to tell me the antidote. It was the red cylinder."

"She has a real temper at times, just like her mother." Harry shrugged. "But, you never get anywhere in this industry if you're nice."

The silence of the spacious ward was broken by the occasional beep from the medical equipment and the hiss from the mask. The glass windows looked out onto the wet streets below. Even several flights up, the glare of the headlights refracting through the glass and up off the porcelain tiles irritated Sean's vision. He pulled a knife from his belt and moved toward the old man.

"Does she want me dead?" Harry asked.

"I'm sorry. I normally wouldn't, but she's poisoned someone who doesn't deserve to die. She's not part of our world."

Harry raised his hand. "There's no need. Talk to me for a while."

"I don't have long."

"Neither do I," Harry replied. "What is Jaide doing?"

"She's keen on moving into weapons. Almost psychotic about it."

Harry shook his head, the disappointment apparent. "I know. It's a foolish move. Those players are a whole other level of crazy. I don't know why she can't see that."

"Ambition, perhaps." *Maybe she's one of them.*

"Who do you work for?"

"The Captain."

"The *Fleet* man." Harry smiled as he hissed the word. "You know that Jaide and the Captain used to go out together?"

"Really?" The revelation surprised Sean. His antagonism toward her had never hinted at anything more than a deep-seated loathing. Perhaps that had been his way of hiding his past.

Harry continued. "Yes. It must have been twenty or more years ago. He was so fond of her."

"That's all touching, but I have a friend dying. Could you tell me where I can get an antidote to the poison in the red cylinder?"

"Could you get me my wallet?" Harry pointed to the flat brown case on the side table. Sean reached out and placed it in Harry's lap. Harry opened the wallet, his fingers fumbling with the delicate leather, and extracted a crisp one-hundred-dollar bill. He folded it and handed it to Sean.

"Bribe?" Harry asked.

Sean shook his head.

"I didn't think so. I'll leave it for the nurse. She has been helpful."

Harry placed the note on his bedside table, and removed another piece of paper, doubled over, from the wallet. He offered it to Sean. An old piece of paper from an old man. It could either be prophetic or blackmail. It was an old photograph, faded and patchy. A younger Harry stood to the left. In the center was Jaide and on the right was the Captain. Young Jaide looked the spitting image of Amanda.

"Jaide thought the Captain was weak. It broke his heart and made him the man we see today. The funny thing is, she never replaced him with anyone else. Couldn't stand him, couldn't live with anyone else. Between you and me, I've never understood the logic of the fairer sex. It is the magic ingredient that makes them so special."

Sean handed back the photograph. Harry stared at the image. "Seeing the two of them together reminds me of quieter times. Dying men often confess their regrets. Do you think we'll be forgiven for what we've done?"

"By God or by family?"

"You don't strike me as a religious man," Harry remarked.

Sean shrugged. He hadn't come for philosophy. "Family matters the most. Forgiveness in their eyes is both the hardest and the greatest achievement. Redemption, on the other hand, is another story. You need to make peace with yourself and your maker, if you are a religious man."

"And if I'm not?"

Sean gazed over the chaotic life humming down on the streets. "You look into the eyes of enough dying men, you learn to find something. I believe you had faith at some point."

Harry turned his head and followed Sean's view out the window. "Are you looking into the distance? Or for a clue to salvation?" He returned his attention to Sean. "You can learn plenty examining your own reflection. Another layer to the ever-increasing hypocrisy by which we live our lives. You are right about the faith. It was once important to me. The reflection doesn't lie. You look at yourself and wonder what you've become."

"You learn there's a cost to everything, both good and bad," Sean agreed.

"I have a last wish." Harry took another deep breath from the oxygen mask. "Do you think you could bring peace?"

"Probably never. But I'll ask around for you. What venom is in the red cylinder? That might convince me."

Harry laughed. "Jaide needs to be less dramatic. It's for hunting. I used to shoot animals out in Africa, Rhodesia when

181

it was called that. It's just tranquilizer."

Sean rolled his eyes. His heart softened. He wondered if he could spare the old man a few moments of peace, to place himself in an appropriate frame of mind. Harry wasn't the kind who raged into the light, an excessive life having taken its toll.

Harry closed his eyes and went quiet. The heart-rate monitor stopped its monotonous beep and tumbled into an uninterrupted shriek.

"Harry. Hello?" Sean shook the old man. His body didn't respond. One problem was solved. He took out his phone and snapped a photograph of Harry with the flatlining monitor in the background.

Rubber-soled shoes squeaked as the medical staff approached. Sean backed into the shadows of the corner, stepping into the en suite bathroom, and recorded the nurses' attempt to resuscitate Harry.

The minutes crawled past and the intensity around the bed dissolved. The head nurse pulled the bed sheet over Harry's head, and the staff left the room. Sean sent the image and footage to Jaide's number as he waited for the ward to quieten.

He then slipped out into the empty corridor. A young male voice shouted behind him. He didn't turn and ran for the door.

15

D UMO AND JENNA examined the CCTV image. The hospital security officer skipped back to the beginning and paused it as the tall foreigner glanced up at the camera. It was O'Reilly, again, and with another body.

"He killed Harry?" Dumo asked.

"No. Harry died of natural causes," the security officer replied.

"He wasn't injected with poison, or the machinery wasn't tampered with?"

"The man was old. A nasty shock could have killed him. There were no signs of trauma or irritation."

"O'Reilly—a killer—turns up but doesn't kill the man. What was he doing?"

"Saying good-bye?" the security officer suggested.

Dumo looked over the young man. "They're hardly friends. He's a Fleet man visiting the head of the Ravens. I have a long list of possibilities, with a double-cross at the top."

"You think he was a Raven working with the Fleets in secret?" Jenna asked.

"Or the other way around?" Dumo suggested. "I'm not sure, but I think something big or momentous is going to happen. That's what our overseas friends said. Neither will be good for us."

The footage continued to play, and then O'Reilly was gone, invisible to the vast network of security cameras throughout the building.

"I'd love to know how he does that," Dumo muttered.

Jenna stared at the display, her face contorted in concentration. "He looked up at the camera."

"So?"

"He knew the camera was there. He's generally been avoiding surveillance. Surely, that means he wanted us to know he was here."

Dumo dropped into silence for a moment as his face blackened. "I'm sorry. I don't think this has a simple answer. Could you play the video again?"

The security guard started the footage rolling again. Jenna squinted as she watched the images flicker past.

"He has a gun in his hand," she said, pointing at a black blurred object. His arm flicked to the side. "What's this bit?"

"What do you mean?" the guard asked.

"His arm just shot out to the side, like he was—" She pointed at the screen. "Take us to this camera."

The security guard led them through the bleached corridors until they stood under the camera. Jenna searched the wall. Blu-tacked to the wall was a slip of paper. She turned it around. It was a photograph—the one of Jaide and the Captain in happier times.

Jenna handed it to Dumo. "Fleet and Ravens, together. Now who do you think O'Reilly works for? Are you sure the voice on the phone was American, or only pretending to be?"

"We traced it. You traced it. It checked out," Dumo replied.

"A major agency would be able to mask their location."

"With our budget, we don't have a hope. We're being played for fools. It's time to bring O'Reilly down. Friends in high places can protect him, but he has to face up to the laws he's broken. Put him on our MOST WANTED list."

"You know what could be worse? What if the people talking to you from overseas aren't the 'good guys'?" Jenna wondered.

*

Sean approached the hotel that served as Jaide's base of operations. Dark-glass walls glowed across the fascia of the abandoned building. It was one big place for one lady. Across the expanse between the road and the building, the guards in their dark uniforms and peaked caps patrolled along the front, armed with semi-automatic weapons and wearing bulletproof vests. They were too far away for a reliable shot. They'd see him coming and mow him down before he was halfway across the promenade.

The humidity bounced along at maximum, crying out for the rain to break the oppressive weather. The clouds hung heavy, and sweat rolled down Sean's forehead. He moved farther down the street and around to the rear of the building. The narrow alley stank of garbage. Cats yowled at one another over the rotting remains discarded in the dumpsters. Dim lights concealed his movement down the alleyway toward the service entrance. Two guards stood, talking to each other while scanning the area. Sean kept tight to the wall until he was close enough to hear them.

"If they can get the old head out of the way, then they've got some new alliance in place."

"But do you want to join them?"

Sean slipped out his Beretta and slowly aimed it. The statement concerned him. A couple of raindrops fell, spotting the ground. *Who would the Ravens be teaming up with and why?* Two quick shots and both guards lay on the ground. Sean ran in and scooped up a cap to hide his face.

The dull gray corridor ran through the services area with the dim lighting adding a sense of confinement. A dripping pipe made the only sound. Sean kept his head down as he passed the security cameras, hoping the cap would give him a few minutes' grace before they either recognized him or noticed the dead guards and worked out he was inside. The stairwell door opened without a sound, and Sean ran up the stairs to the fourth floor. His footfalls made no sound on the luxury carpet in the empty corridor.

He glanced into the meeting room. A black raven cutout hung ominous in the gloom as a deep red neon light glowed from behind, illuminating its edges. *It's late, where is everyone?*

From the outside, the lack of lights indicated hardly anyone awake in the building. That left down as the only option.

Sean took the sleek lift down to the basement. The lift's doors opened into an odorous concrete corridor. He opened the first door along the hall to reveal stacked wooden crates. He was opening a second door when the door handle at the far end of the corridor turned. He crept along the wall, keeping flat against the concrete and out of view. Voices floated out into the hall. Sean kicked the door. It crashed against a man as Sean barged into a cold storeroom, causing him to reel back into another. Chanchai lay on a metal table.

The first man, still in shock, withdrew a knife and lunged at Sean, expecting him to retreat. Instead, Sean stood his ground and grabbed the man's knife, twisting the man's wrist and wheeling him into an arm lock. Sean stripped the knife out of the man's grip and sunk it into his opponent's neck. Blood fountained as the man reeled backward, clutching at his throat.

The second Raven, the larger of the two, leaped on Sean and rammed him against the wall. Sean swung his elbow around, grazing his attacker, who then hooked his arms under Sean's shoulders and clasped his fingers around the back of his neck. Sean flailed his arms behind, but failed to snag a hold. He relaxed and reclined into the man's grip, forcing the Raven back under his weight until the man lost his footing and stumbled backward. Sean stiffened and drove his head up in a reverse headbutt and the two fell, with Sean landing heavily on top of the Raven.

The man bounced up onto his feet, grabbing a scalpel off the table. Sean picked up a steel tray and deflected a lunge, swatting aside his attacker's hand. He then swept the tray up and into the man's throat. The edge jabbed into the soft flesh. Sean tripped the Raven and brought down the tray against his head as they landed on the floor. Sean rolled, grabbed the scalpel and speared it into the man's throat.

Shouts echoed from outside. They must have found the breached security. Sean scrambled up and rifled through Chanchai's clothing until he found the phone. Low battery and a weak signal, but it was enough. He pulled out a small piece of paper from his back pocket and dialed the number written on it.

"Tom?"

"*Yeah.*"

"Sean here."

"*You took your time. Did you track down Amanda?*"

"She didn't make it. Someone got to her first."

The line went quiet. Several seconds passed before Tom replied. "*Who?*"

"Whoever used the phone I'm calling you on. Can you pull the info on it—owner, address?"

"*Will do. Give me ten minutes.*"

The shouts grew louder.

"Call me back on this number." Sean hung up and crept out toward the corridor.

Voices floated through the doorway. Sean slammed the great steel door as the guards crashed into the far side. He rammed the bolt closed, sealing himself inside. The room had no other exits, save for an air vent in the ceiling. The hammering on the door increased then was replaced by machine-gun fire. Bullets sliced through the metal and into the flesh of the fallen men inside. The guards battered the door until it finally bent and buckled.

Sean's options were limited. The air vent seemed to provide the safest escape, and there was no chance of disguising its use. He pushed Chanchai off the table and climbed up. Dust rained on him as he levered the grating open.

*

Lindsey paced in the cell. Her head had cleared from the initial surge from the poison, and she'd become pointedly aware of the passing time. Jaide had said she had little more than two hours. It'd been well over an hour, and Sean hadn't returned. Lindsey was sure, as part of the poisoning process, that her head was playing tricks. Her muscles twanged, and dizziness and nausea overwhelmed her. Perspiration dripped from her forehead. She strained to breathe in the stifling heat. The air-conditioning duct creaked and groaned, but nothing fresh came out. Metal walls and a tiled floor spotted with blood surrounded a large steel drain in the center of the room.

She'd heard muffled gunfire five minutes ago, but nothing since. She hoped Sean wasn't on the receiving end. The air vent let out another cacophony of grinding and crashing metal. The grating on the air vent flew open, smashing down into the ground.

*

Sean crashed to the floor and rolling onto his back. He blinked up at the lights. Lindsey stood over him.

"Did you get the antidote?" she demanded.

"I'm fine. Thanks for asking." Sean rose with difficulty and dusted himself down. "It wasn't poison, just a tranquilizer."

She sagged in relief, her face flushing as the release drained her body. He caught her around her waist. She pulled him closer.

"Do you remember what you saw when they brought you in here?" Sean said.

"It's a bit blurry, but I think there was only one guard standing at the entrance. He had a machine gun across his chest."

"Facing which way?"

"The gun? Toward his left shoulder."

"Anything else out there? Chairs, bulletproof armor?"

"Um, I don't think so. We came through a kitchen. I remember the smells of cooking." Lindsey held her stomach. "I've just remembered how hungry I was. You owe me dinner. You got anything I can nibble on?" She gave him a hungry expression.

"The tranquilizer may be clouding your judgment," Sean said. He gave her a sideways look as he pulled himself back into the air vent.

He crawled along, glancing down through the occasional grating. The armed security officer stood at attention by the entrance to the kitchen's preparation area, just as she had described. Sean smashed down on the vent and jumped onto the guard as he turned at the noise. Sean landed on his shoulders, his weight dragging the man down. The two tumbled onto the ground. Sean stood, grabbed the guard, and punched into his jaw, rendering him unconscious. A set of keys jangled loudly as Sean lifted them off the guard's belt. He ran to the cell and unlocked the door.

"Quick," he hissed at Lindsey. "They're on to us."

She came toward him, so close there was barely a hairsbreadth between them. She looked up into his eyes. Her own were still full of innocent enthusiasm, but now they hinted at something else. Sean felt as if he was being targeted, but in a less aggressive way. "I'm still hungry," Lindsey whispered before moving past him toward the doorway.

Sean returned her smile as they exited the cell. He could smell the light rose of her perfume mixed with her sweat all the way down the corridor. She certainly had taken to adventure. Back in the corridor, voices could be heard in all directions.

"How can we get out?" Lindsey asked.

"Through the foyer," Sean replied.

"The front door? This isn't one of those plans that is 'so stupid they wouldn't possibly do it.' Because history is full of dumb plans leaving lots of people dead."

Sean went to speak one thing, then thought better of it. "Trust me."

"Trust the spy?"

"I said I'm not—"

"Yeah, yeah. You deny everything. I did not have sexual relations with that woman." She caught Sean's expression. "It's a figure of speech, not some fantasy for you to … mull … over."

Sean led the way. They emerged out of the stairwell into the foyer. It contained over a half-dozen people. Six men in the Ravens' security uniforms stood waiting. A figure disappeared around a corner. Jaide stood smiling in the center of the room.

"She must really mean something for you to come back," she said.

"Your father is dead. I've got the girl. Some people got hurt. Your odds are running out. Will you let me walk out of here?"

Jaide laughed. "Your impudence is, at least, entertaining. Double pay to whoever kills him."

Sean assessed the situation. Six armed men were evenly spread around the room. His odds weren't good. They needed to make a mistake, and he needed to be quick. He shifted his weight from foot to foot, keeping focused on the men. No one had a gun on him yet; could he pull his own before they could? Probably not. One Raven stepped in close to his side. He was, with a stretch, within reach. That will be the mistake.

"Who's going to be first?" Sean coaxed.

The farthest man on the left tensed then moved, reaching around for his pistol. Sean lunged to the right, grabbing the closest man, dragging him near. The farthest man fired as Sean spun and used the man between him and the gunman as a human shield. The bullet passed through the Raven's head.

Sean drew his Beretta and fired at the next two men. Two taps to each head. Three down. The next shot went off target, and another man charged at Sean from the left. Too close to fire. Sean dropped to his knees and jabbed the man in the crotch. The guard bent over. Sean brought his pistol around and fired up through the man's head, spinning him up and into the path of another attacker carrying a long butcher's knife. Sean aimed at that man and fired, landing a bullet right between his eyes. The last remaining attacker slashed down with the recovered butcher's knife.

Sean dodged, kicking the Raven's leg, forcing him off balance. Sean caught the knife arm, reversed the blade and rammed it through his attacker's stomach. The man collapsed, gurgling as blood poured out of his mouth. Sean kicked him away and faced Jaide. He raised his gun to aim at her head.

He took a deep breath, trying to recover. "I'm going to say this once. You can probably guess that I'm the kind of guy you should take seriously." Sean moved around to face her. "Confirm that you understand this."

Jaide's eyes flicked from the pistol aimed between her eyes to the bodies scattered over the floor. She nodded, her bravado gone.

"Your departed father wanted one thing. Your safety. This is a violent occupation, there needs to be peace or at least an understanding. I'm suggesting to you, at gunpoint, to back off from the Fleet. Come up with some truce. Heal the past. I don't care. It was his last wish, and it will be your mercy."

Jaide was about to speak when Sean's cell rang. The screen displayed Tom's number. "Hold that thought, I've got to get this."

He lifted the phone to his ear while watching Jaide. Lindsey moved to his side, maneuvering through the dead men. "Tom, yeah, what have you got."

As the information came in, his face darkened. Words failed him. He lowered his gun and stared at Lindsey, his face unreadable.

"All fucking bets are off," he finally said.

Lindsey stared into his face, her eyes radiating concern. "Everything all right?"

"No." He slipped the Beretta back into his belt and ran out of the room. "I'll come back for you, Lindsey." Sean then pointed at Jaide and said, "Touch her and I'll rip out your throat."

16

FRACTURED LIGHT FELL through the tall windows like daggers, piercing the shadows in a patchwork across the wooden floor. The Captain's office had transformed in the dark, full of hidden and dangerous corners.

Sean pulled open the safe behind his boss's desk. Inside was the scarf Amanda had been wearing in the footage from her bedroom. Another folder was attached. It contained a fax itemizing a weapons list with pricing from Hydra, signed by Ichkeria-six. *FOUR will be in contact* was scrawled at the base of the note. The paperwork was dated the day after Amanda's death and marked *Delivery: ASAP*. Everything was being fast-tracked. Sean stood and turned, clutching the scarf. Anger welled within him, drowning his vision in red.

"Sean, what in the name of the devil are you doing here?" The Captain stepped forward into the room. His entrance had been silent.

Sean studied his employer in the darkness. He raised the scarf, thrusting it toward the Captain. "Why'd you kill Amanda?"

The Captain riled, rising up to his full height. "What is it to you? What is *she* to you? Did you ever love her?"

"She was a friend. A good person, not one of us. She didn't deserve to die." He struggled to keep his rage under control.

"Who are you to say who deserves to live or die?"

"Don't twist my words. I'm asking why *you* killed her."

"She didn't respect me."

"Was it because she reminded you of Jaide? I saw the photo

of her as a young girl. She and Amanda looked the same."

"Don't mention that bitch around me. Jaide called me weak when I would have done anything for her. I loved her true and deep, and she just threw it away and stabbed me in the back." The bitterness in the Captain's voice disturbed Sean. He'd never seen his boss so emotional. Sean spared a moment for the Captain's sorrow. Behind all the words, he was just another man with a broken heart.

"But Amanda wasn't Jaide," Sean said.

"That's what I was hoping for. But what would you know? You, who is afraid to show who you really are, locking away everything about yourself."

"I lock away those things to keep the ones I cherish safe. I do it for them, not for myself." Sean rubbed the scarf between his fingers. "Life doesn't have to be dominated by greed. It'll only disguise your true nature." He shook the scarf at the Captain. "I always knew you were pretty low, but this is something else. You didn't even have the backbone to use your phone, using Chanchai's instead. You're all cowards, stealing each other's phones because you're afraid of the people at the other end knowing it's you and not answering."

"Don't you—of all people—lecture me. Take care of him," the Captain shouted before he turned and left.

A shadow moved across Sean's peripheral vision an instant before someone, a young man, lunged at him. Then, from the opposing side, another body appeared. They both had close-cropped hair and were feral with aggression, wild-eyed on an amphetamine cocktail. Sean was pinned between the attackers.

The side doors burst open, and a third, older man ran into the room. The two young men were on Sean, raising expandable batons, even as he was turning to face them. Sean dropped into a combat roll, pulled out his Beretta and managed one shot, sending one of the men spinning into the wall, clutching his shoulder. The baton rattled across the floor. The older man stepped in and kicked Sean's wrist. The savage impact sent the Beretta skipping into the shadows. Sean lunged after the metal bar. A kick landed in his stomach.

The older man stood back, pacing around the conflict, as the remaining young man launched a frantic attack. Sean darted to the side and flung the man aside with a hip toss. The young man fell in a tangle, and Sean mounted him, pummeling with both fists. The older man stepped in again and lashed out. Sean caught the movement out the corner of his eye and rolled out of the way. A second blow grazed Sean's temple as he managed to snap out of the reach of older man. The younger man climbed up. Sean grabbed the free baton, then in one movement, spun up and smashed his baton against the one of the younger man.

The clattering of the metal bars rang out, deafening those in close range. The older man kicked into Sean's hamstring, forcing his leg to crumple. A roundhouse kick then sent Sean crashing out through the French doors. The glass and wood shattered, blowing out onto the small garden. Sean dropped, picked up a piece of glass, then stabbed it into the chest of the older man, who fell away with blood pouring down his shirt. Sean's final attacker grabbed him around the throat and dragged him back into the room, punching Sean repeatedly in the lower back.

The kick came in at head height. Sean had seen the attack in the man's eyes before he'd moved and parried the blow with his forearm, then grabbed his attacker's leg and pulled the man in close. Sean felt the anger flow, releasing it and letting his body perform unfettered by emotion. He twirled around on the ground with broken glass crunching under his body. The attacker twisted his leg and kicked up, aiming for Sean's head. Sean easily caught the maneuver, intercepted it, then leaped up and slammed the man to the ground. Before the young man had time to breathe, Sean had hoisted him up and thrust him through the French doors out into the small garden and backward onto a decorative cast iron spike on the fencing.

Sean ran back into the room, picked up a baton, and continued searching.

*

The Captain was nowhere to be found. Sean heard a car in the garage start, and charged out through the rooms. The Captain's Mercedes pulled out in the street. Sean smashed his fists on the trunk, but the car sped away.

An old Ducati motorcycle sat nearby, semi-concealed under a dust sheet. Sean pulled away the sheet, revealing a set of gloves resting over the instruments of the red beast. The ancient electrics were easy to hotwire and the engine ticked over. It spluttered, then died. He tried again with more choke and the engine roared into life. He straddled the seat, collapsed the baton, and slipped it into his pocket before he pulled on the gloves. The engine growled as Sean twisted the throttle and accelerated out onto the roadway.

The rain lanced down, stinging Sean's eyes. He wiped away the rain, but the oncoming headlights disorientated him. The Mercedes raced ahead, weaving through traffic. It lurched between the lanes, the taillights barging between the other vehicles.

The Captain gunned down the long stretch on the Sirat Expressway. Bangkok shrunk away in the haze of monsoonal rain, its grimy lights resolving into nothing more than a gritty glow.

A gap appeared in the traffic, and Sean pulled up the motorcycle beside the Mercedes. He reached down and grabbed the steel baton from his pocket with his right hand and threw it in the air, catching it in his left, and smashed it through the driver's window. The glass shattered and rained down over the Captain, startling him. He swerved to the right, forcing Sean to flick the bike out of the way with the one hand he had on the handlebars. The motorcycle bucked under the urgent steering. Sean slammed on the front brake, fumbling on the clutch with his left hand, and the rear wheel lifted into the air. The momentum spun the motorbike on the spot as he rammed his foot into the ground to stop it toppling to the side. The wheel came down, grating the tire against the Ducati's mudguard, and Sean twisted the accelerator to full. The motorcycle tore off in pursuit of the Mercedes again as it sped along the bridge.

The Captain had drawn alongside a haulage truck and kept pace with it, protecting the open window. Sean maneuvered the bike in behind the truck, attempting to keep out of view. But the spray being thrown up off the road made it impossible. He pulled back out and gunned the motorcycle between the truck and the Mercedes. The Captain swerved to the right, smashing into the motorcycle. Sean grabbed the car's roof, the jagged remains of the window cutting into the gloves. He flew onto the hood and smashed the metal bar into the windscreen.

The Ducati twisted and buckled under the car as the motorcycle was dragged along the bitumen, throwing up a fountain of sparks. It caught the car's axle, slowing down the Mercedes and lurching it to the right. Sean threw himself off the hood. He landed and bowled along the road, using the gloves to protect his head, a row of trash cans lining the street cushioning his impact. The front of the Mercedes dragged into the truck. The car dove into the ground, the front plowing into the tarmac. The bumper and grill were ripped off and under the truck's wheels.

The car rolled, the ends crumpling as it tumbled. It smashed into a streetlamp and came to rest. Metal creaked and groaned as the Mercedes cooled. The radiator blew. Steam billowed from under the crumpled hood. One turn indicator flashed intermittently. The truck shuddered and jolted as the driver slammed on the brakes, coming to a stop fifty meters down the road. The cars behind pulled up quickly as the Mercedes's wreckage caught on fire.

Sean eased himself up. He ached from head to toe. His left forearm throbbed, and his fingers were numb. The gloves were shredded. He limped over to the car and wrenched open the door. The Captain fell out, covered in the white dust from the airbag. Sean hauled up the diminutive man and drew back his right arm for a punch. Pain stabbed through his arm, forcing him to drop the Captain.

The Captain seized Sean's arm and twisted, causing him to cry out in pain. He followed with a swift kick to Sean's ribcage, knocking the wind from him. Drivers appeared from the stalled cars, with one or two carrying crowbars and wheel braces.

The Captain charged toward Sean, clutching at his injured arm. The pain kept Sean off balance, and the Captain pushed them to the side of the bridge. The two tumbled over the barricade and fell into the river.

They thrashed in the water, grappling at each other as the current dragged them along. As the water sucked them down, they separated and pushed for the riverbank. Sean crawled up on his hands and knees, with the Captain emerging a dozen meters down.

They both rose on unsteady legs and circled, assessing each other. Lightning flickered across the sky, highlighting the muddy ground.

Sean tried two quick jabs, but the Captain dodged the blows with legendary speed.

"You should learn to recognize when you've been beaten," the Captain said.

"It's not over," Sean replied.

"You don't know what you've thrown away. With Hydra, we could have ruled the city. I was finally going to get my chance. Harry Gabat kept me down for all those years. Their family showed no loyalty. No honor."

"Loyalty? Honor? You sell drugs."

"But it could have been so much more."

The Captain charged, grabbing Sean around the waist. Sean stumbled in the mud, fighting for balance. His foot caught in the mangroves, allowing him to spin and throw his attacker wide. The Captain recovered and delivered several lightning blows. Sean took the punches to his torso, then hooked the Captain's arm under his left arm. Two punches from Sean and the Captain fell to his knees.

Sean floored the Captain with a kick. He caught the glint of metal in the Captain's hand and sprinted for the water before the Captain could shoot. The small pistol misfired. On the third attempt, a shot rang out.

Sean felt a burning in his shoulder. He rolled into the gloom near the river's edge. The Captain was up and searching along the bank. He then paused, waited, and listened. The waves lapped at the shore and the current gurgled.

Up out of the mangroves, Sean rose. The uppercut caught the Captain by surprise, landing flush on his jaw. The Captain was lifted off the ground and landed on his back.

Sean placed his boot on the small man's chest. The gun barrel caught the streetlights, and Sean wrenched it out of the Captain's hand. People shouted from the bridge. A helicopter approached.

"You think you can buy some kind of salvation?" the Captain shouted. "You're damned forever, just like the rest of us."

"You think this is about redemption? This is revenge," Sean replied.

He cocked the gun and aimed it.

"For Amanda."

Sean pulled the trigger.

17

THE CHAOS OF the previous day felt distant, and Henderson found herself strangely deflated. A new dawn, a new day full of possibilities. There had been plenty of information for her to process. Then, first thing in the morning, another piece of information landed in her lap from an unexpected source.

"A fax has been sent to us," Henderson told Banks after she strode into his office.

"A fax?" he replied. His office had a bad smell to it today, as if he'd slept in it overnight.

"Not a fax, per se, but a photo of one. A weapons list from someone called Ichkeria-six. You heard of them?"

Clive shook his head.

"And for a group called Hydra," Henderson continued. "I don't suppose you've heard of them, either."

"No."

"Neither have we. I ran the name through the database and nothing came up. Which is odd considering we have *everyone* on the database."

"Perhaps they're new."

"Yeah, perhaps. My major concern is that it mentions an agent. FOUR. FOUR was with Brad at the time he went dark."

"Who sent the fax, or the picture of the fax?"

"Sean O'Reilly."

Banks chuckled. "The person who we think is a traitor has sent us information? And you want to believe him? He could be simply trying to cause this exact kind of confusion."

But Henderson wasn't laughing. "Perhaps. But, looking at it from an IA perspective, there is enough contradictory information for a deep investigation."

"How did we get tangled up with Sean O'Reilly? Who brought him in?"

"Tom Robinson."

"Has he turned up anywhere yet?"

"No."

"For Christ's sake. Get some momentum on it."

Henderson rose and left for the logistics room, still in early-morning shock.

*

Banks picked up the phone and pressed the top left button. His blood pressure was building to the point where he could feel the pounding in his head. Again, the line switched through to voice mail.

"I don't know what you're playing at, but I'm suggesting you remember what's at stake," he said into the phone. "Henderson is getting close. We need to eradicate her enthusiasm one way or another. And why have I heard nothing from Four? If this is one of your political games it will end badly."

Banks replaced the handset as a tall woman knocked on his door. "Yes?"

"Hi," she said with a smile. "Jane Madison from IA. One of my juniors was down yesterday."

"Yes, yes. Most inconvenient. What is it?" He turned his attention to the folders scattered across his desk.

Jane closed the door behind her. "There are a couple of items I'd like to discuss with you. If it's not too *inconvenient*, of course."

Two suited men positioned themselves outside the office,

backs to the window and scanning the corridor.

*

"Verity," Henderson said as she entered the crunch room. She was carrying two oversized coffees from the canteen. "O'Reilly has been in contact with me."

Palmer bolted upright. "Really?"

"He's highlighted an organization called Hydra and someone called Ichkeria-six. You heard of either?" She handed Palmer a coffee.

"No. Do you want me to search?"

"I've already tried, but nothing's in the database. I think he's sending us a message. According to yesterday's findings, we betrayed him. So, why would O'Reilly do anything for us?"

Palmer waited for her superior to process the thoughts. They sipped at their large coffees.

"Is he trying to tell us something?" Palmer asked. "Like, follow Hydra or Ichkeria-six."

"The man is an enigma wrapped in a riddle. He had an accent, didn't he?"

"Yes. Irish."

"An Irish man from the Foreign Legion and the CIA. Those are specialized career choices. Who made him the man he is? What did he do before the Foreign Legion?"

"We don't have access to that."

"Who is our focal for the Legion?"

Palmer glanced around. "It's me."

Henderson sat down and lowered her voice. "I need to talk to someone who has access to their historical records."

"Is it to do with the Bangkok situation?"

Henderson nodded. "I've got to get to the bottom of who Sean O'Reilly is. But more importantly, I think it's to do with us. Something is rotten."

201

"Once IA, always IA?" Palmer replied. She then wrote a name on a loose sheet of paper and slid it over to Henderson. "This will cost me."

Henderson glanced over the scrawl before folding it and placing it in her shirt pocket. "Intelligence agent?"

"Paris at night is not a particularly dangerous or lonely place for a single girl. You never know who you might meet."

Henderson scooped up the papers and slipped them into a manila folder, tapping the edges into alignment.

"Jane from IA is putting some heat on Banks. He may crack. I'll be back."

"Where are you going?"

"To the Foreign Legion."

"In Corsica?"

"I'm calling it a long overdue holiday," Henderson called back over her shoulder.

*

Ice rattled in two crystal tumblers. The light caught the edges and formed a prism across the desktop. It felt odd to Sean to see someone else behind the Captain's desk. Charlie was the antithesis of the Captain's taste and culture. The magnificence of the oak and the craftsmanship of the ornate carving would be lost on him. Something too old and tatty to have any real value. But that was Charlie. Hasty reparations to the demolished French doors exposed his total lack of taste. A cheap PVC replacement had been installed in their place. Hideous, cheap and nasty. Just like Charlie.

The weapons list from Hydra sat on the table between them.

"Like a whiskey?" Charlie asked.

"A water will be fine," Sean replied.

"Still or sparkling?"

"Sparkling. I'm feeling brave."

"You done good with the Captain. Showed good judgment. aide was impressed, too."

"Jaide?"

"Yeah, she's me new partner."

Sean sighed. "You've joined together?"

"We've been working on this Kolokol gas deal for ages, but her old man was the sticking point. You know how these locals get about their loyalty to generational hierarchy. Republicans through and through. Thanks to you, he's out of the way." He walked over to the bar. "You said he wanted peace? Well, as it happens, we're going to get peace between the Ravens and the Fleets, just not in the way Harry imagined."

Sean thought back to the old man and shrugged. "I don't think he would have minded."

"And blow me down if you didn't get rid of the Captain at the same time. It was getting right messy with everyone double-crossing and backstabbing one another. It was almost as bad as being out in the Middle East. Anyway, it's over. You fixed it right good. A complete masterstroke."

Charlie smiled and squirted a stream of fizzing water into another tumbler. He slid it across the table toward Sean.

The phone on the desk rang, and Charlie picked up the receiver. He chatted away, glancing over at his guest. Sean spun a large globe and watched the world pass by. He slowed it and placed his hand on Ireland. Charlie replaced the handset and stood behind Sean, noting where his hand was.

"You want to go home?" he asked.

"Aye. But I can't, let alone even talk to my family," Sean answered.

"This"—he handed over the telephone handset—"is an anonymous number."

Sean shook his head. "They're always listening."

"I know some people. If you join us, I'll talk to them. See

what we can arrange." Charlie sipped from his tumbler, the ice knocking around in the remnants of the drink. "You in?"

Sean turned and stared deep into the man's eyes. He was as trustworthy as a vicar's daughter on her eighteenth birthday. But it had been the only sniff at going home he'd had.

"Aye," he replied and downed his own drink. "But I need to find out who Ichkeria-six is."

Charlie shrugged. "Indeed. Could be our best customer. Always handy having inside info. To the future and anonymous benefactors."

Sean considered the man's face. The glance away when making a statement. A subtle scratch of the ear. A nervous swallow. He'd had a lifetime in undercover; he knew how to read the enemy.

Charlie knew the identity of Ichkeria-six.

18

HENDERSON SWATTED AWAY the flies as she stepped off the train at the Calvi station. The idyllic ride from Bastia across the Mediterranean island revealed breathtaking scenery. If she put away enough money, this would be the dream location for her retirement.

Her cell buzzed. Texts from Palmer. The first one had her laughing out loud. From a casual inquiry, IA had found a thread. When they pulled, it unearthed information Banks couldn't explain. He'd blamed Williams, but she'd gone dark. Banks was stonewalling, but Williams' disappearance was a trigger. He may even break by the time she was back. Henderson pocketed her phone and continued on.

Where would someone like Williams be able to hide? She

wasn't a shrinking violet. She had around-the-clock protection and surveillance.

Henderson had met Williams three times, and each time it had been an unpleasant battle. If it hadn't been the unquestionable delegation from the CIA Director, and his personal appearance on one occasion, Henderson doubted she'd have gotten in the door. Queries over authority, the actual usefulness of the investigation, last-minute cancelled meetings. The list of deceptive practices took up pages and yielded little information. You might as well strangle the breeze.

How do you challenge someone with a Grade-A security clearance and had dined with the president? And reminded you of that. But, why would Williams hide? She only had to wave her get-out-of-jail-free card.

Henderson strolled up the cobbled medieval streets from the train station with the majestic Mediterranean sky rolling out in all directions, punctuated by the citadel, Columbus's rumored birthplace, against the infinite blue carpet. The gorgeous Calvi Bay curled around to the alpine mountains on the opposing side. It was off-peak tourist season and a tranquility radiated out of the few locals peacefully ambling around the town. A town famed for the police, military police, the mafia, and the French Foreign Legion, this was probably the safest place on the planet. It would take a brave person to cause any trouble in this paradise.

Henderson checked the address on her cell. The map led her toward the monolithic castle, then off into the network of small alleyways crawling around the base, then to an ancient building with a plain stone facade, an old wooden door, a rusty street number cut out of old steel, and little else. She turned the door handle and stepped into a clean and modern reception area cut into the building's structure. Clerical staff, who manned a series of desks across the room, typed in near silence. A row of old metal shelves lined one wall and contained a combination of files and abandoned computer equipment. A reception bench stretched from one side to the other with an iron gate secured into the wall.

The sergeant sitting behind the bench recoiled in surprise.

Henderson struggled through several set French phrases prepared by Palmer before the soldier gave her a withering look.

"We speak English here as well. But thank you for the ... effort. You are wishing to enroll?"

"No, I'm looking for Lieutenant Gerard." She waved away an errant fly attempting to enter her mouth. Jet lag sapped her energy. "I have an appointment."

The soldier checked his computer monitor and nodded. The gate to the side buzzed and clicked. He indicated for her to go through.

"Third door on the right," the sergeant said, holding up three fingers.

"It's okay, I speak English, too." Henderson followed the old stone corridor. A junior on his knees swept the floor with a hand brush. The dark rings under his eyes and the smell of stale alcohol explained the situation.

She counted the three doors, then double-counted as her mind settled into the fog of jet lag before knocking. A gruff voice answered, beckoning her inside.

"Lieutenant Gerard?" Henderson asked.

The officer smiled and nodded his head. "That is me." His thick accent was barely understandable.

"Thank you for seeing me, Lieutenant." Henderson entered the office and closed the door behind her.

"You have come a long way. Coffee? You look tired." Gerard indicated the visitor's chair, and she slumped into it.

"My body is telling me it's three in the morning. So, strong and black. Thank you."

The lieutenant punched a button on his handset and issued a quick order for two black coffees. He returned his attention to his guest.

"Did you have any luck with the information I sent through?" Henderson said.

"Your message was vague, but if the CIA is prepared to come all this way to discuss something, then I assume it is important."

"I need to be careful what information is transmitted outside the agency when it's this sensitive. I'm hunting down some history about Sean O'Reilly, a former agent of ours who we originally sourced from the Legion. Our data on him suddenly seems a little sketchy, so I'm hoping you can fill in some details about his past."

"I'm not sure what you may gain. I'm sorry, but if that is why you are here then you will have a wasted trip. I can't tell you anything."

"Palmer works for me. She said you could be persuaded to help."

He squirmed in his seat before nodding his head. "I wondered how long that would take to come back to me." He sighed. "Paris nights can carry their own cost for a single man. This can be our only conversation. Then you must tell her we are even."

He pulled up a file on his monitor, making sure Henderson couldn't see. "What did you want to know about him?"

"Can you tell me his real name?"

"Sean O'Reilly. It is his real name."

"Aren't people meant to get a new name?"

"No. Perhaps decades ago, on extremely rare occasions for operational reasons. But it would be our choice for our own military benefit. Not for the convenience of an individual."

"Like what?"

"If we were commissioned to remove a rogue senior military head who had an extreme ideology and we needed a soldier in close. Even then, it wouldn't be a completely new name. It would be similar. As an example, Sean O'Reilly might get a passport with the name Sean Reilly. Or Simon O'Reilly. You say he was an agent of yours?"

"Yes."

"Before he joined us?"

"No. After. We engaged him four years ago from here," Henderson said. "After being ten years with you."

Gerard glanced back at the monitor. "No. That is not possible. The official records state he … er, *left* the Legion nine years ago." He paused as he glanced over his glasses and read the page. "And he, without any doubt, did not join the CIA." The lieutenant pursed his lips and shook his head.

"Are you saying …" She paused, placing her head in her hands. "What are you saying?"

"There is empirical proof that he could not, and did not, join the CIA."

"No, there must be a mistake. We recruited him from the Legion. We have it documented in exacting detail. Photographs, recordings, everything." She pulled a thick file out of her carry-on satchel and placed it on the desk.

Gerard flipped through the file, then shrugged. "I don't know what to tell you as you don't seem to want to believe the facts. One thing strikes me. These are excessively detailed records: what people ate, when, where. How much. Is this kind of detail typical?"

Henderson paused. Through her exhausted mind, connections were being missed. "No, not to my knowledge."

"Isn't that peculiar?"

Henderson placed her head in her hands again. Gerard closed the folder and slid it back. He glanced at the monitor again.

"Wait. The task leader is a friend. One moment." He picked up the phone and spoke quickly in French lilting with an Italian accent. He then returned his attention to Henderson.

"Where did he sign up?" Henderson asked. "He was Irish national."

"The records show he joined at the Paris branch." A smile danced across Gerard's lips as a memory caught in his eyes. "Clean record. No warning signs."

"No, again that is conflicting with our records. He had an incident as a child, killed a boy when he was seventeen. Ex-IRA."

"I feel I must explain how the Legion operates in the twenty-first century. When you join, you must present your official papers. We do thorough background checks on everyone. If you have any felonies, such as murder, on your record, you are unacceptable to the Legion."

Henderson leaned forward on the desk, confusion etching into her face. "Then we have the psychological tests. Somehow, Mr. O'Reilly managed to slip through that net."

"I can't believe this," Gerard asserted. "It doesn't mesh with any of our facts. What do you mean 'slipped through'?"

The door opened, and a middle-aged and well-built captain stepped into the room. His face was tanned and scarred.

"Captain, this is Sandra Henderson from American Intelligence," Gerard said. The captain gave Henderson a curt but polite nod. "Ms. Henderson, this is Captain Christoph. He was CO of the team that contained Sean O'Reilly."

Christoph made a sound that showed he wasn't happy hearing the name. He crossed his arms over his barrel chest. "Gerard, are you still in for the squash match?" Gerard nodded. "Good. Now what do the Americans want to know about O'Reilly?"

"Do you remember him?"

"Yeah, I remember him. Had to court martial the psychotic bastard personally," Christoph replied.

"Court martialed? Is he still in jail?" Henderson asked.

"No. It was out on the African plains. When you get a soldier who flips out, it has to be a bit more immediate and final, especially when, well, when you do the kind of things he did. Pardon my language, but nine years ago, I put a bullet through the fucker's brain."

Henderson dropped into silence, staring at the captain.

"No, I'm sure this is all wrong." She pulled the profile shot from the folder and handed it to the captain.

"Interesting. This is not Sean O'Reilly," Christoph confirmed.

"Then who the hell is it?"

*

Lindsey rested her head against Sean's chest. Her leg folded over his body and kicked off the bed sheet. A ceiling fan blew a weak breeze, cooling the thin veneer of sweat.

Shadows cast from the setting sun stretched across the room. He'd watched them elongate over the last ten minutes. A sigh of contentment escaped Lindsey. A Cheshire Cat-like smile spread across her lips.

"So what now?" she asked.

"Does there have to be anything?" Sean replied.

"We could go to Rome."

He smiled, then shook his head.

"Paris? There are plenty of cities to explore in America."

Sean laughed. "I've got a few things to find out."

"Are you going to hunt down Ichkeria-six?" She stared up into his eyes and stroked her fingers across his jaw. "Do you know who it is?"

"That is top-secret information. And no, I don't know who it is."

Amanda's retribution hadn't played out as he'd expected. She'd opened a real can of worms. And Sean couldn't let it go.

Ichkeria-six floated before him every time he closed his eyes. Who else would know? Other team members? Did Tank or anyone from the early days know? It was a deep secret, and someone had used it. What concerned him the most was that *someone* may be using it to send him a message.

He ran his fingers over Lindsey's body. They'd spent the day naked and her bronzed and toned body had been something to behold.

"I've been meaning to ask you about your running. You seem to have the fitness level of an elite athlete."

"Huh?"

"You could run like the wind. How did you get so fit?"

"I guess some of those old military exercises paid off."

"That can't be all there is—"

The phone rang.

"Who's that?" Lindsey bolted upright. Her breasts bounced in front of him, derailing his thoughts.

"It's Charlie. He's set up a call with me ma."

Sean sat and stared at the phone, letting it ring.

"Go on, answer it," Lindsey said.

He reached for the handset and noticed his hand was trembling.

She grasped his hands in hers, and kissed him. "It's going to be all right. I'm here."

Epilogue

THE MESSAGE ARRIVED out of the blue one Sunday morning. Only one person knew her little superstition of checking each cap before throwing it away. At first, she thought it was a cruel prank, but *no one else knew*. Secreted in the red screw top was a small piece of waxed paper, folded over and again. Her heart had nearly burst as she unfolded the paper and read the message. She held her breath, afraid she'd blow away this distant and impossible chance.

The phone in the living room rang, and her head snapped around. Her heartbeat soared as she approached the decades-old relic. It continued to ring as she reached out and lifted the yellowing handset out of the cradle.

"Hello?" she said, her accent so thick it was incomprehensible outside the region.

Silence. Like there always was. Tears welled in her eyes.

"Is that ..." she started, then stopped herself as she recalled the instructions in the bottle cap.

She sat down in the collapsing old sofa with the receiver burning against her ear, smiling and softly crying, and joined in the silence.

Lightning Source UK Ltd.
Milton Keynes UK
UKOW01f0709290317
297789UK00004BA/123/P